KEN GREENHALL was born in Detroit in 1928, the son of immigrants from England. He graduated from high school at age 15, worked at a record store for a time, and was drafted into the military, serving in Germany. He earned his degree from Wayne State University and moved to New York, where he worked as an editor of reference books, first on the staff of the *Encyclopedia Americana* and later for the *New Columbia Encyclopedia*. Greenhall had a longtime interest in the supernatural and took leave from his job to write his first novel, *Elizabeth* (1976), a tale of witchcraft published under his mother's maiden name, Jessica Hamilton. Several more novels followed, including *Hell Hound* (1977), which was published abroad as *Baxter* and adapted for a critically acclaimed 1989 French film under that title. Greenhall died in 2014.

By Ken Greenhall

Elizabeth (1976)*
Hell Hound (1977)*
Childgrave (1982)*
The Companion (1988)
Deathchain (1991)
Lenoir (1998)

Ken Greenhall

ELIZABETH

A Novel of the Unnatural

WITH A NEW INTRODUCTION BY
JONATHAN JANZ

VALANCOURT BOOKS

Elizabeth by Ken Greenhall
First published by Random House in 1976
This edition first published 2017

Copyright © 1976 by Ken Greenhall
Introduction copyright © 2017 by Jonathan Janz

Published by Valancourt Books, Richmond, Virginia
http://www.valancourtbooks.com

ISBN 978-1-943910-67-0 (trade paperback)
Also available as an electronic book and forthcoming as an
audiobook

All Valancourt Books publications are printed on acid free paper
that meets all ANSI standards for archival quality paper.

Cover by Henry Petrides
Set in Dante MT

INTRODUCTION

Elizabeth: An Unnaturally Forgotten Novel

The subtitle of Ken Greenhall's sublime *Elizabeth* is *A Novel of the Unnatural*. The word *unnatural* is uniquely suited to this book, for as you'll find within the first few pages, there's something unnatural happening in the Cuttner family. Exacerbating this unnaturalness is the uncommonly talented author telling us this story, an author who has been criminally neglected by modern readers.

I should warn you of something, however. There's also something unnatural about the eponymous star of this novel.

I find myself musing on Greenhall's title, that single name: *Elizabeth*. Part of me wishes he'd called the book *The Cunning Folk* or *The Woman in the Mirror*, but I suspect Greenhall didn't want to shift the reader's attention from his main character.

He needn't have worried.

Elizabeth Cuttner is one of the most fascinating characters in fiction. To say I was transfixed by her musings (filtered through Greenhall's eerily rational prose) would be doing the character a disservice. *Mesmerized* comes a little closer but doesn't get us all the way. *Exerted an inexorable gravitational pull* probably comes the closest. I started *Elizabeth* one night before bed and found myself antsy the following day to return to Greenhall's strange world. And once I did return, I read until well past two in the morning to learn what would become of Elizabeth.

This brings us back to the title. In a just world, the title *Elizabeth* would be as iconic as Daphne du Maurier's

Rebecca. But alas, we know our world is far from fair, and we know some authors rise to canonical levels (like du Maurier, who deserved it) while some (like Greenhall, who also deserved it) don't.

This is why I'm so excited about Valancourt's new edition of Greenhall's book.

Before you begin this classic—no, it's not considered a classic yet, but after reading it, you'll help the novel achieve the status it deserves, won't you?—I need to divulge a few truths. I'd feel guilty if I didn't prepare you for them. You see, unlike Elizabeth, I do feel guilt.

The first topic for which you need to prepare is the subject matter. Early in the novel I was reminded of Nabokov's *Lolita,* and if your discomfort (or revulsion, or indignation) toward that sort of plot is extreme, you might give this novel a miss. Mind you, it's not *exactly* like *Lolita,* but there are echoes of that story here, at least with regard to the age of the title character and the adult situations in which she's embroiled. Furthermore, those who are put off by sensuality, violence, and aberrant familial relationships need not apply.

Concerning the book's sensuality . . .

There's a lot of it. But what's so fascinating is the manner in which Greenhall insinuates rather than displays, what he conveys via the brush of a hand or a downcast gaze. What he leaves to the imagination.

Folks, this story *seethes* with eroticism, though not always of the healthiest sort. While young Elizabeth is certainly at the center of the tale's carnality, through her eyes we're made to understand how very important sex is to the other characters in the cast. Matters of sensuality are ubiquitous in *Elizabeth,* yet it's remarkable how effortlessly Greenhall suggests sexual acts without employing protracted explanations. In fact, the entire novel is a model of efficiency. The result is a story that's over before it's begun, and isn't that one of the highest compliments one can pay a book—that the reader wishes it were longer?

The final facet of *Elizabeth* I'd like to mention is Greenhall's artistry. This, friends, is a writer who chooses words with delicate precision, who somehow renders the most indelicate acts and subjects darkly beautiful with his craftsmanship. Here are just a few of the passages I highlighted and will be returning to again and again to remind myself of what can happen when supreme skill meets spellbinding subject matter:

> In the night I would hear the slopping of the lake against rocks, and half-awake, I sometimes mistook it for the sound of someone choking.

Or this:

> I reached down and grasped the hem of my wrinkled nightgown and pulled it over my head. I looked again at the mirror and then shivered and moved away, feeling as though a stranger had been looking at my body. I enjoyed the feeling.

And one more:

> Their backs were to me, and Mother was making sardine sandwiches. Her hands glittered with oil, and she was carefully lining up the little headless bodies on dark bread. She raised a finger to her mouth and slowly licked it. She was standing too close to James. She was a desperate, gross woman, and I wanted her desperation to increase.

This, folks, is Ken Greenhall. Clear, elegant, chilling. And unexpected. Which is one of the many characteristics that distinguishes this tale from others. One mark of a great storyteller is the ability to surprise the reader, but to do so in a way that, upon rereading, feels like it was inevitable.

Ira Levin had that power. So did Richard Matheson. Stephen King has it too.

We know these names, and we rightfully celebrate them.

It's time to start celebrating Ken Greenhall.

Elizabeth is a marvelous place to start.

JONATHAN JANZ

JONATHAN JANZ is the author of twelve novels and numerous novellas and short stories. His work has been lauded by *Library Journal*, *Booklist*, and *Publishers Weekly*, as well as being championed by authors like Brian Keene, Jack Ketchum, Edward Lee, and Tim Waggoner. He enjoys his other life as a teacher of English, Creative Writing, and Film Literature, but his heart belongs to his wife and three children.

ELIZABETH

One

When Grandmother vanished, the glass of the large, handsome mirror in her bedroom was found scattered on the floor in small, glittering pieces, like the remains of a collapsed, bleached mosaic.

Have you ever thought about mirrors? Maybe you have. In your bathroom, perhaps, on a quiet Sunday night while you were performing one of those personal acts that you never speak of. Perhaps you were cutting the hairs that grow in the moist darkness of your nostrils. The only sound was the snipping of the tiny scissors.

I hope you are not embarrassed to have me speak so frankly to you. Remember that I am no longer a child; I am a young woman. My mirror tells me so, and the eyes of men tell me so. When I was younger I saw James, my father's brother, look from our dog to me without changing his expression. I soon taught him to look at me in a way he looked at nothing else.

But I was speaking of mirrors. Have you thought of how you depend on them? Would you be convinced of your beauty or your unconventional attractiveness if your mirror didn't reassure you so many times each day? Perhaps you are being deceived; your skin may not really be unblemished; the sensual, unbroken curve of your lower lip may be flawed by a slackness on one side. There is really no way to know whether your mirror shows you what others see or what is really there.

If you have thought seriously about mirrors, you will know about their mystery. If you were to go into your bedroom tonight—perhaps by candlelight—and sit quietly before the large mirror, you might see what I have seen. Sit quietly and patiently, looking neither at yourself nor at the glass. You might notice that the image is not yours, but that of an exceptional person who lived at some other time.

★ ★ ★

My name is Elizabeth Cuttner, and I am fourteen years old. I know you would be more interested in my story if I were a middle-aged person, but I ask you to remember what you were like when you were fourteen. Is there a chance that you were more perceptive then than you are now? Almost certainly you were passionately interested in something then. What is your passionate interest now?

I'll admit there are many things I know very little about. But there are many things I do know. I know, for example, that you recently sat watching television with someone you are supposed to love and that you thought neither of that person nor of what you were watching. Perhaps you thought longingly or regretfully of something that happened to you when you were fourteen.

I think I know how the world seems to you. That might not have been true two years ago, when I was a girl. But as I have told you, I am a woman now, and there is no feeling you have had that I have not had. It is possible that I have had important experiences that were denied you. I think you will come to believe that.

I first came to live with Grandmother about a year ago, after I killed my parents. I don't mean to sound callous. Let me explain.

Two

Mother and Father had taken me for a vacation to the family cabin at Lake George, New York. The cabin had always seemed mysterious and fascinating to me. I was especially interested in the disturbing marks left by former inhabitants: puzzling stains; the small hole in the bathroom wall, stuffed with brittle, yellowed tissue; cigarette burns on the edge of the varnished pine table.

In the night I would hear the slopping of the lake against rocks, and half-awake, I sometimes mistook it for the sound of someone choking.

I decided to surprise my parents that morning by serving them breakfast while they were still in their damp, thin-mattressed bed. I was awake at dawn, and I lowered my feet onto the cold floor, feeling the roughness where feet had begun to wear away the varnish. I walked slowly across the room, and in the gray light of the room I saw an unexpected movement that startled me for an instant before I realized that it was my reflection in the old rust-edged mirror that hung above the dresser.

It was then I first heard the voice that later became familiar and important to me. But the voice was so distant and gentle that I thought it was an illusion caused by the shrill wave of birdsong that had begun with the dawn.

I paused before the mirror. My eyes were half opened, and I touched their outer corners and felt the small crusty deposits that had formed there in the night. I reached down and grasped the hem of my wrinkled nightgown and pulled it over my head. I looked again at the mirror and then shivered and moved away, feeling as though a stranger had been looking at my body. I enjoyed the feeling.

"Breakfast. I've brought breakfast."

My parents had not been asleep, and their surprised expressions were tinged with both gratitude and annoyance. Father rubbed his hand across his pale cheek, and I could hear the hiss of whiskers. He had not yet had time to assume the expression of confidence and energy he liked to show, and I saw him as Mother and I knew him to be. There was a row of pink scratches across his chest.

Mother was flushed. She raised the sheet to cover her breasts. She and Father wanted me to believe there was nothing shameful about the human body, but all three of us knew better.

There should have been a ray of sunshine to glint on the runny yolks of the eggs I had fried, but there was no sun that day. I took the tray and laid it across their thighs. I went to Father's side of the bed. He put his arm around me and pressed his gritty cheek against mine. As he kissed me I matched my fingers to the scratch marks on his chest. His breath was sour with last night's whiskey. Father had what Mother called a drinking problem and what he called a gusto for living.

Mother pushed the corner of a piece of toast into an egg yolk, releasing the warm, bright liquid. We all smiled, but no one spoke. I realized the birds were quiet now, and a wind had risen.

I walked in the woods that morning. I have always liked solitude, and there is a special excitement about being surrounded by the non-human. Perhaps you think of things that live in the woods as pleasant. I don't know how you can believe that. It may be that you don't look carefully, and see only chipmunks and daisies. What of the moles and mushrooms? I saw both that morning. The mole was dead, and its delicate fur was swarming with ants. The mushrooms were a brilliant orange, and they glowed almost phosphorescently in the half-light that penetrated the thick summer foliage of the trees.

In our woods there are also signs warning of rattlesnakes and giving instructions on how to treat snakebites. I stopped to read one of the signs, aware of the hidden life surrounding me, and I wondered what I would see if I stood up and turned over the rock I was sitting on.

I was not far from the cabin, and from the sounds I heard, I knew that Mother was washing the breakfast dishes and Father was taking a shower. Cheap, mismatched dishes clacked against the kitchen sink, and the uneven spray of the stall shower rumbled against thin metal walls.

My parents were both singing. I don't think either of them knew a complete song, but they knew hundreds of bits, which they worked into confusing collages. Most of the words were about love. As far as I could tell, my parents didn't love each other, but like many people, they felt they should. I have never seen the necessity for love.

I was about to start back to the cabin, when something moved on the ground in front of me. I paused and looked down at the damp, yeasty-smelling earth and its covering of decaying vegetation. A moment later there was another flash of movement, and I found at my feet the most arresting creature I had ever seen. I decided it must be a toad. It was the color of decaying meat, and it was marked with blackish-green warts. I picked it up. I felt as if I were holding the hand of a dead dwarf. The toad didn't struggle, but sat staring at me with eyes that resembled tiny peeled grapes. We watched each other for a few minutes, and I could feel its heart beating against my hand. My own heart was beating quickly, out of an excitement that seemed at first to be fear. But as I watched the creature resting calmly in my hand, I realized that I was not frightened. I pressed the toad gently against my chest, and it seemed as though our hearts were beating at the same speed.

I could not let the toad go, despite its ugliness. It made no effort to escape me, and I decided to take it back to the cabin.

Father stood on the porch, staring across the lake at

Tongue Mountain. He was wearing bathing trunks and holding a glass of whiskey. The mist that had obscured the mountain was lifting. The wind was cool, and the flat grayness of the sky was becoming blotched with black clouds. Father shivered. His skin was yellowish and lifeless, and I thought of rows of chicken flesh displayed in a market. His legs were thin, and a roll of flesh gathered at the top of his trunks. Did he realize how unattractive he looked?

He saw me and smiled. "How about a canoe ride?" he asked.

"Yes. But first I must put this away." I held out my hands and showed him the toad. Father walked toward me and looked at what I held. He was frightened, as I knew he would be. He drank some whiskey and asked, "Aren't you afraid of getting warts?"

"No. I'm going to keep it as a pet."

Father looked at me solemnly. I tried to imagine what he was thinking. It was something I often had to do, because he hid his thoughts. Father was a stockbroker, and he once told me that the secret of selling stocks was the ability to distract customers from unpleasant truths. Perhaps he was right, for he earned a lot of money. But I thought it must be easier to avoid unpleasant truths in business than it is in other areas of life, for I had seen him stumble and vomit. And I had watched him touch Miranda, my school friend.

The screen door slammed, and Mother appeared. "What are you two doing?" she asked.

Father looked relieved. "Our daughter has captured a beast."

Mother was wearing sandals, and as she came across the porch I was reminded that her feet were her least attractive feature. I liked to imagine that the twisted toes and horn-like bulges were the result of someone's having tortured her when she was a young woman.

Mother was fascinated by the toad. "How cute," she said. "What are you going to do with it?"

"She's going to wait until she's alone," said Father. "And then she's going to kiss it, hoping it will turn into a prince."

It was something I hadn't thought of, but when Father suggested it, I knew I would kiss the toad. I would not be thinking of princes, though.

"How exciting," said Mother. She put her face close to the toad. "I don't suppose you'd want to share him with me," she said.

Father was annoyed. "Why is it that beautiful women are always attracted to ugliness?"

Mother smiled at him. "Isn't it fortunate for you that we are?"

She was playing her favorite game. The point was to say something cruel in a teasing, smiling way. If Father was offended, it showed he couldn't take a joke, and he lost the game.

He knew that the only way to keep from losing the game was to smile and return the insult. "Oh, I didn't mean you, dear," he said. "I was talking about *beautiful* women."

Father never won the game, because unlike Mother, he seldom meant what he said. It was Mother's turn. She said, "Your opinions about beauty lack authority, darling—as do all your opinions except those on commerce and alcohol."

Father laughed, which meant he had been defeated. I hated Mother for starting the game, and I hated Father for losing it.

"Can we go for a canoe ride now?" I asked.

Father was glad to change the subject. He looked out at the lake, which was creased with white-peaked waves. "I think it's a little rough for that, Elizabeth. Maybe this afternoon will be better."

"You didn't think it was too rough five minutes ago."

"It's much rougher now."

It wasn't any rougher. It was just that Mother had depressed him. He wanted to sit and drink. "I think I'll go and put some more clothes on," he said. He drank what was left in his glass and went into the cabin.

Mother watched him with a pleased expression. She said to me, "Why don't you go and find a home for your toad, dear. There are some empty boxes in the closet. I'm going down to the dock."

I thought she was probably going for a canoe ride.

It was dark in the cabin. Father was in the bathroom. I went into my bedroom, closed the door, and put the toad on the dresser. It had not moved since I picked it up. The wind outside was steady now, and as it moved against the trees, it made a sound like heavy breathing. I stared at the toad. And I spoke to it: "Do you have a name? Would you have a name if I kissed you?" It didn't move. I picked it up and held its cold, warty skin to my cheek. My hands enclosed its body, and I pressed its head gently to my mouth.

The wind seemed louder, like a nearby unending gasp, and as I parted my lips slightly and pressed them against the toad's belly, I heard a name being whispered. Core? Gore? Yes, it was Gore.

My heart was pounding, and I once again felt an urge to place the toad against my chest. But this time I unbuttoned my blouse. I placed the creature gently between my breasts, and I felt the tiny cold feet touch my skin. I raised my eyes to the mirror, and there in the dim, stormy light I saw a face that was not mine. I closed my eyes and heard my name spoken in a whisper.

"Elizabeth. Look at me, Elizabeth."

I opened my eyes. The image in the mirror was unclear, but I was certain it was not mine. I stared at it for some moments, and slowly a feeling of terror grew in me. The face before me was smiling tentatively. It was not a young woman I saw, but someone perhaps the age of my mother: a woman with dark hair parted in the center of her head and pulled straight back. The face was surrounded by darkness, and I could not see her body. She might have been wearing a black robe.

I heard her voice again, although her mouth did not seem to move. "Do not fear me, Elizabeth. I have come to help you. Do you believe that?"

"Yes."

"Call me Frances."

"Yes, Frances."

I don't know what I thought as I answered the voice. But despite what I said, I was afraid. I shuddered and remembered the toad. I put it down on the dresser and pulled my blouse closed. As I did so, the image in the mirror faded, and I began to see my own pale, shocked features.

The voice had faded too, but I could still hear it. "Elizabeth," it whispered. "Do not reject me."

I had moved away from the mirror, and the voice stopped.

You don't believe what I have just described, do you? Yet you believe that men have walked on the moon; that they have left bags of urine there to freeze in the bleak shadows. I don't mind if you want to believe that I have imagined things. I don't mind, because I know there is a part of you that would believe me if you would let it.

Three

"Is there anyone home?"

It was the voice of James, my father's brother. James had strong, tanned legs. His waist was muscled, and I had never seen uncertainty in his eyes. He was my lover.

I went into the sitting room. Father was not there. James stood alone on the porch. I had been afraid his wife and son might be with him. We were separated by the screen door, and although I could see him clearly, I knew he could not see through the screen into the darkness of the cabin. I moved close to the door and whispered, "James."

The wind was still strong, and he did not hear me. He called again: "Is anyone there?"

There are few things more enjoyable than watching someone secretly. I have done it often, and I believe that most people exist only when they know someone is observing them. It is like the tree that falls unheard in the forest— the unheard sound does not exist. The unobserved person usually does not exist either. That was not true of James, however. He had a strength that increased in isolation.

"James," I whispered again. His eyes focused on the door, and he smiled.

I placed my hand against the screen. I knew how it would look to him: splayed, white, and dismembered.

"Are you alone?" he asked.

"Mother and Father are probably at the dock."

A hook dangled at the side of the door, above a little splintered arc it had worn in the wood. I raised the hook and pushed it through the screw eye on the door frame.

James pulled at the door handle. "It's locked," he said. "Open it. I want to touch you."

I stepped back from the door and waited to see what James would do. I suppose you think I was being childish, but it was more than that. James liked to perform little desperate acts. The circumstances of his life were purposely odd and messy, and they forced him to behave desperately. That pleased him, and I liked to add to his pleasure.

James raised his leg and kicked a hole in the middle of the screen. He reached through the bulging, jagged tear and unlocked the door. As he entered the cabin I turned my back to him. He came up behind me and put his left arm across my breasts and bit my neck. His right hand was under my skirt. I was pleased.

We found my parents at the dock. Father was angrily dragging a canoe out of the boat shed.

James shouted, "Hi." Father had forbidden me to use that word. He said it was only fit to be used by women on television commercials. Father wanted me to be a superior person.

"Jim," Father said. "What are you doing here?" He looked angrier than ever.

Mother, who had been slumped in a beach chair, pulled her shoulders back, crossed her legs to reveal a blue-veined thigh, and smiled.

James looked politely at her thigh and then into her eyes, pretending he had seen something pleasant. "I had to drive Katherine and the boy to her mother's," James said. "The old woman can't stomach me, you know. So I thought I'd stop by here and say hello. I brought some stuff for a picnic."

Father turned his back on us and tugged at the canoe. The squeal of aluminum dragging across raised nail heads on the dock mingled with the sound of the wind.

Mother frowned at Father for a moment and then got up and walked toward James. "What a lovely idea, Jim. We'll take the canoe out to one of the islands."

"It's too rough to go that far," Father said.

Mother took James's arm. "Jim and I will get the food ready," she said. "Help your father with the canoe, Elizabeth." She and James walked away toward the cabin.

I sat down and watched Father struggle with the canoe. I heard Mother's aggressive laughter in the distance. James, I knew, disliked the sound of her laugh, as he disliked the lines that laughter produced in her face.

"I don't need you here," Father said. "Why don't you help your mother?"

He probably didn't want her to be alone with James. Father didn't realize that almost no one shared his attraction to Mother.

Or perhaps he only wanted to be by himself. Father was never comfortable with me, particularly not since I had become a woman. I think it was his discomfort with me that first made me aware of the power that comes with womanhood. What did he think when I walked at his side and took his arm so that I could brush it against my breast? I believe he felt some combination of the arousal that I brought to James and the fear I produced in boys at school.

Perhaps Mother was now holding James's arm. Perhaps her laughter was so harsh because she realized that the power of her womanhood was leaving her. It was the only power she had ever known.

I would not make the mistakes that Mother had made. I thought of the mirror and of the pale image of Frances, who said she would help me. I would know more than one kind of power.

Father had pushed the canoe into the water.

"Where shall we go for the picnic?" I asked.

"I don't think you should come with us, Liz." He only called me Liz when he was angry with me.

"Why are you angry?"

"I'm not angry. It's a dangerous trip, and you can't swim."

"You and Mother can't swim either."

"We're more experienced in the boat than you are."

"You're angry because Uncle James is here."

Father was trembling. He stood with the dark-treed mountain behind him. In the sand at the edge of the water I could see the footprints of a small, sharp-clawed animal. Yesterday Father had eaten lunch in a Manhattan restaurant, warm and familiar. The hatcheck girl had smiled and spoken his name.

"You're not coming with us, Liz. You can stay in the cabin and read."

Father was being sarcastic. Once he had come into my bedroom and found me running my fingers over the cloth binding of a book. The cloth was white, and the title of the book was stamped in gold. He had taken the book from me and placed my right hand in one of his. He had run my fingertips over the hair on the back of his other hand. "You read too much," he had said. It was a night Mother said she had to play bridge, and he was distressed.

Father enjoyed distress. He stood on the dock, his sneakers wet from water that had spilled from the canoe. If he had put his arms around me and told me he wanted me to go with him to an island, I would have rubbed his pale feet with my hands, smoothing the puckered skin and ignoring the traces of dirt under his toenails. But because he was engrossed in his distress, I wanted to increase it. I turned away from him.

As I walked back to the cabin I remembered that I had left the toad on my bedroom dresser. Gore. Would he still be there? I opened the torn screen door. How had James explained that to Mother?

They were in the kitchen, talking about food but thinking, I was sure, about something less innocent. Their backs were to me, and Mother was making sardine sandwiches. Her hands glittered with oil, and she was carefully lining up the little headless bodies on dark bread. She raised a finger to her mouth and slowly licked it. She was standing too close to James. She was a desperate, gross woman, and I wanted her desperation to increase.

Gore had not moved. I picked him up and sat on the edge of the bed. I was facing the mirror, but I did not look into it. After a few moments I heard the sound of heavy breathing, and then the whisper: "Elizabeth, look at me."

I raised my eyes and saw Frances clearly for the first time. She was younger than I had thought at first: perhaps thirty years old. Her hair and eyes were dark and her skin pale. She had a strong but uncared-for face. She wore a coarse-woven linen dress.

"Do you see me clearly, my dear?"

"Yes."

"Do you understand why you see me?"

I could not answer. The image had assumed a gentle expression, and I began to realize how attractive Frances was. I wanted to touch her.

"You see me because we are kindred," she said. "I have come to teach you things about yourself. I have come to offer you powers. Will you accept?"

"Yes, Frances. I think so."

"Those around you will misunderstand your powers, just as mine were misunderstood. My body was examined and abused. So may yours be. You must welcome it." Frances' voice had become gentle. She spoke in what seemed to be a British accent, but it was unlike any I had heard before. "Accept my mark," she said.

I felt something touching me. I looked down. The short skirt I was wearing was raised high on my legs, and resting on my right knee was a spider. It moved slowly up my thigh, black against the white skin. I wanted to strike at it, but my hands were cupped around Gore and I could not open them. I remembered how, earlier, James's hand had moved up my leg.

"You have chosen," said Frances.

The spider stopped, and I felt a brief, stinging pain where it rested. I moved my hands toward it, the toad's tongue flashed out, and the spider was gone. In its place was a small scarlet mark that resembled a character from a strange language.

"Elizabeth?" It was Mother calling to me from the other room.

I looked into the mirror. Frances was smiling gently, but her image was fading. "Gore will do your bidding," she said. And then she vanished. I saw my own flushed face. I was smiling too.

"Elizabeth, are you there?" The door opened, and Mother stood in the doorway. There were creases across her forehead. "What have you been doing?" she asked. "You look strange."

"I've been feeding my toad. I found a spider for it."

The lines in her forehead deepened. James stood behind her. He was looking at my thigh.

"Well, you play with your little friend," Mother said. "We're leaving for our picnic."

"You won't take me?" I asked.

"No. It's not safe."

"Why not bring her along, Sheila?" James said. "I'm a strong swimmer. I'll look after her."

James would have liked to be in the water with me, our clothes clinging to our bodies, our hands grasping, with the dark, insubstantial water below us. But he would not say more. And Mother would not relent. "I'll let you look after *me* instead," she said. She should not have said that.

"I'll come down to the dock with you anyway," I said. I dropped Gore into my blouse and walked behind them. The path among the trees was crossed with roots that had been revealed like large, pale veins where the soil had been worn away. James and Mother carried the picnic basket between them like a little coffin. Gore's cold body pressed against my stomach. The woods were darker than ever.

It was scarcely lighter when we emerged onto the dock. Father was sitting in the canoe, holding a bottle. He smiled up at us, obviously not liking anything he saw. But he decided to be pleasant. "All aboard for the deluge. But no minors," he said.

"Aren't you taking life preservers?" I asked. He wouldn't do it now that I had suggested it.

"No. Just umbrellas."

"We'll be all right when we get to the islands," Mother said. "There's shelter there."

Father came up to help load the canoe. I went to the edge of the dock and reached into my blouse for the toad. I dropped it into the front of the canoe, whispering, "James is not to be harmed."

Father and James got into the canoe. They both helped Mother down from the dock. The slack flesh of her arms quivered as each man took one of her hands. She was laughing, absorbed in her own pleasure. Father and James sat in the ends of the canoe. Mother sat in the middle, turning without hesitation to face James.

As the canoe moved away, only James waved to me. It was then that I realized what would happen. Mother laughed again, still deep in pleasure. Her final pleasure.

As I stood watching the canoe move unsteadily across the gray water, I became aware that someone was watching me from among the nearby trees. I turned toward the woods and recognized Mr. Hurlbut. People didn't like Mr. Hurlbut. He knew when the ice would break up in the spring, and his wife screamed in the night. Although he was probably about my grandmother's age, I thought of him not as an old man, but as a young man who looked old. He was the only person I knew who didn't bathe very often. I admired him.

"Hello, Miss Elizabeth."

I waved.

"Your folks are making a mistake going out in this weather," he said calmly.

"Yes, I know. They like to make mistakes."

"Wasn't that your Uncle James with them?"

"Yes."

"I think of him as a careful man."

"I don't think of him that way. But he's a strong swimmer."

Mr. Hurlbut nodded, compressing the dirty creases in his neck. "I'll patch that screen door for you," he said. One of the reasons Mr. Hurlbut was disliked was that his expression seldom changed.

I turned and started back to the cabin.

I sat on the porch and waited for someone to walk solemnly up the path to tell me that my life had been changed. Behind me, in the cabin, the mirror was reflecting a lifeless pine-paneled wall. Wind, dampened by the lake, pushed against me and lifted my skirt. I saw the strange red mark on my leg, and I began to tremble.

It was much later when I looked up again. James and Mr. Hurlbut stood before me. My hands were desperately grasping the arms of the chair. Mr. Hurlbut stared at me with an expression that could have meant either accusation or sympathy. James's wet clothes clung tightly to his body. A drop of water rolled from his matted hair, down his forehead and cheek and past the corner of his smiling mouth.

Four

That is how I came to live in Grandmother's house. It was built in 1836 and contains twenty-three mirrors. The one I was fondest of was in the attic and was made many years ago in England.

James also lived in Grandmother's house. He often met me in the attic, and we would lie before the mirror on a dusty half-rolled rug. I had not told James about Frances. He did not know that she watched us and that as she did so she whispered again and again a list of unpleasant words. She and James told me often of the pleasure I brought them. I felt something other than pleasure.

I sometimes thought of James's wife and son in the room beneath us. They were easily embarrassed, and they tried to love me as one should a new daughter and sister.

Grandmother appeared only at dinner and spoke only of things that happened before she was born. Many years ago she did something that caused her husband to leave her in despair. He had not seen or spoken to her since, but she continued to bear his name and share his wealth. He was Jonathan Cuttner. His offices were in the building adjoining ours, but he never visited us.

The Cuttners had been ship's chandlers since the family first came to America in the eighteenth century. They supplied and sustained generations of merchant seamen. James knew how such men live. He had lain awake at night, hearing steel plates strain against the force of the dark water. He had smelled the stale grease of the galley and seen the cook cough up blood. He said men at sea perform acts that would be unacceptable to any other group of humans.

Our address was 46 Coenties Slip, and we had no neighbors; at least not in the usual sense. During the day the streets were busy with workers: exporters, ship brokers, and others who had offices in the few blocks of four-story Federal-style buildings that had survived with ours. Each year the skyscrapers of the financial district extended closer to us, and we were walled against the waterfront by a forty-story curtain of glass and metal.

But at night the life left those buildings. The workers deserted them, heading farther up Manhattan or across the rivers, leaving the Cuttners alone with the harbor and the cats that slunk through the dark streets.

You will have a better idea of how we lived if I describe the way we took our evening meal. Dinner was served at seven o'clock. By that time the streets were quiet, and the house asserted itself. It was like a musical instrument that amplified with its old wood the sounds of its inhabitants. We were quiet people, even James's son Keith, who was eleven years old. I believed Keith was sexless, but I was not certain. He collected snakes.

Mr. and Mrs. Taylor lived in the basement. They kept the house clean and prepared the meals. They had an air of innocence. That is a quality I had seldom encountered, and then only in people I didn't know well. I hoped to know the Taylors better.

Before dinner I would sit in the study, which adjoined the dining room. I listened to the sounds from below me in the kitchen, where Mrs. Taylor roasted small animals and pieces of larger ones. From above I heard the muffled sound of James's voice as he spoke to Katherine, his wife. I had no interest in what he said to her. He imagined I was jealous of her, but that was because he imagined I was in love with him as he was with me.

Grandmother entered the dining room each evening at seven o'clock. She always wore floor-length black dresses. Her body was slender and firm, and I wondered what she did in the silence of her shuttered room to keep her skin from growing slack and her muscles from becoming stringy. I wanted her to invite me to her room.

James sat at Grandmother's right, and his wife was

opposite him. I sat next to James, facing Keith, who seldom raised his eyes from the table. At my back, above the fireplace, was a large gilt-framed mirror. I think Keith was afraid to look into it.

Mr. Taylor served the meal, handling the delicate old china carefully and glancing constantly at Grandmother. Before she began her meal, Grandmother looked at each of us as if for the first time. I think she was amused by us, but not enough to maintain a more than momentary interest. She seldom spoke except to deliver precise little accounts of the lives of her ancestors. I thought those stories were lies, but I listened carefully because she often talked of the unnatural.

She said her English ancestors had maintained a country home in the County of Essex during the sixteenth century, and she spoke occasionally of "cunning folk" who lived nearby.

James said he had never heard Grandmother tell the same story twice, and he believed she spent her days composing an imaginary history which she reported to us each evening. As she spoke, her thin lips stretched to reveal soft, glistening bits of half-chewed food.

It was at such a dinner that James told us that an outsider was to enter the house. I knew he was going to say something that concerned me, because he had been staring at me all through dinner as though he were trying to gauge my mood. He had never understood that I have only one mood.

As dessert was being served he said, "Elizabeth, I have some good news for you." That meant he had bad news. "I've arranged to have a tutor come and live with us until you're ready to return to school."

I had refused to go back to school after coming to live at Grandmother's. I had never liked school even though I always received high grades. The teachers and the studying were harmless enough, but the important events at school are those that take place secretly among the students. I was tired of that vicious, giggling world, which was dominated by nothing more profound than menstruation and baseball.

James was smiling apprehensively. He was afraid of what I would say and do the next time we were alone.

"I don't think that's necessary," I said. "I don't intend ever to return to school."

Katherine looked at me patronizingly. "But you're such an intelligent child," she said. "We can't let you waste your talents. And I'm sure you'll change your mind before too long."

I could see she had arranged the whole thing. Keith was smiling smugly. He attended a private school, unhappily and unsuccessfully.

I could see no point in refusing the arrangement. I was sure I could deal with the tutor and could bring the situation to my advantage. I hoped it would be a man.

"Who is the tutor?" I asked.

"Her name is Miss Barton," Katherine said. "She's highly recommended and is especially good about European history. She's actually a distant relative of ours. Your grandmother has corresponded with her about family history."

"Is she an old woman?"

"I suppose you'd think so. But she's younger than I am. About thirty-five, I'd say."

I looked at James. Perhaps I was wrong to think Katherine had planned this. It could be that James merely wanted to have another woman in the house. He needed the constant attention and flattery of women, and he had been delighted when he left his father's business to occupy himself with what he called the management of Grandmother's affairs. He is happiest when a woman is looking at his body, and I wouldn't be surprised if even old Mrs. Taylor had looked up from her work in the kitchen to see him standing before her in an open robe. Her bony hand would have opened in pleasure, letting her carving knife fall to the floor.

"I'm sure you'll get along with Miss Barton," James said to me. "She seems like an uncommonly imaginative person."

I think imaginative people create most of the world's problems, but I saw no reason to warn them of that. I'd let them find out for themselves. "I don't suppose I have any choice," I said.

"We think you should give it a try," said Katherine. "We've arranged to have Miss Barton move in next week on a trial basis. She'll be in the spare bedroom on your floor."

Grandmother had been listening carefully while sipping the cognac she always had at the end of her meal. She said nothing, but once she looked at James in open disapproval. I was sure the day would come when Grandmother would invite me to her room. I knew we had important things to tell each other.

After dinner I went to the attic. James was going to the opera, and I knew he would not be visiting me. James enjoys opera, but I find it vulgar. But as I've told you, James is fond of desperate situations.

I sat on the rug and faced the mirror, awaiting my secret pleasure. Frances spoke to me before she appeared, her voice beginning softly, then gradually becoming rich and clear.

"My Elizabeth is most comely tonight," she said. I had become accustomed to her strange speech, and I cherished the odd words she used.

"As a maiden, I too was comely. And men such as your

James took delight in me. Even the gentry invited me into their bedchambers. You have not seen me as a maiden, have you?"

"No, Frances. May I?" It had taken me some time to realize that Frances was not always the same age when she appeared to me. At first I thought the mirror was distorting her features, but then it occurred to me that the distortions were those of time. I had never seen her looking much younger than twenty-five, however.

"Look, my cony," she said. "Thus I was at your age."

Slowly an image began to form. She was very close to me. There were times when she stood at a distance, so that I saw her whole figure. That night I saw her from the waist up.

As Frances appeared in her later life, she was not quite beautiful, and it was difficult to know whether or not that had always been true. When she appeared as a young woman, I saw that she had once been undeniably beautiful. I wondered what had caused that beauty to erode.

"Are you pleased?" she asked. Her voice was more gentle than I had ever heard it.

"Yes, Frances."

"My only power then was the power of appearance. I bartered that for strength, my dear one." She was wearing a low-cut gown, in contrast to the high-necked dresses she usually wore, and for the first time I saw the wax-white skin of her chest. "Attend carefully," she said.

As she spoke, her face began to change. The tiny muscles that gave freshness and mobility to her features began to soften and sag. Minute lines appeared around her eyes and mouth. I particularly noticed the pale area at the base of her throat, which gradually grew rough and on which there suddenly appeared the same kind of red mark that I had on my thigh. When her mark appeared, Frances' features became fixed, and she was no longer beautiful.

The pleasure that I usually took in being with Frances began to leave me, and I wanted to see myself rather than her in the mirror.

"As you wish, Elizabeth," she said, although I had not spoken my thoughts. Her image was immediately replaced by mine, or by a caricature of mine. I saw myself as I might be in thirty years. My skin was coarsened with the thousand barely visible marks produced by half a lifetime. It could not have been a placid lifetime.

I was more frightened than I had ever been, and as I rushed from the attic, crouched down to avoid the exposed rafters of the low roof, I heard Frances laughing.

In the hallway I passed Keith. He was holding a small bright-green snake, and as I passed him his mouth loosened in what might have been fear. What had he seen when he looked at me?

I ignored him and ran through my room and into the bathroom. I turned on the bright lights and looked into the mirror. I saw myself as I knew myself to be: young, beautiful, and unflawed. I was breathing heavily in relief, and I felt childish for the first time in months—and for the last time.

Five

Three days later Miss Barton arrived. James came to my room that morning, as he often did. He told Katherine he was coming to wake me, but I was always awake when he entered the room. I was never dressed. He would stand in the doorway and say loudly enough for Katherine to overhear, "Time to get up, Elizabeth." I would smile and draw back the sheets. He would kneel at the side of the bed and would sometimes kiss the mark on my thigh. I often thought of my parents and that last morning in the cabin.

When James left the room, reminding me that I would meet Miss Barton at breakfast, I turned to the mirror. I had by then come to realize that Frances would appear only when I willed it or when she had a message for me. As I stood wondering whether to summon her, she appeared. Her image was clearly detailed in the morning light, but she stood at a distance, framed in a doorway. She did not speak, and I watched her for a few moments, aware that there was something disturbing about her appearance. Then I realized she was wearing modern clothing: a gray skirt that reached just below her knees and a long-sleeved lavender blouse.

She spoke one word: "Beware." And then she vanished. I called her back, but the mirror showed me only my own reflection. My eyebrows had drawn together, as they did when I was frightened.

I was not eager to meet Miss Barton. I bathed slowly, not using any soap, but lying in the old marble tub and staring at my body through the tepid, distorting water. I wondered whether I was happy, or whether such a thing was important.

As I finished dressing, there was a knock at the door. I opened it and saw Katherine.

"Elizabeth," she said, "I'd like you to meet Miss Barton."

Katherine stood aside, and a woman appeared in the doorway. She was wearing a gray skirt and a lavender blouse. It was Frances.

"Hello, Elizabeth," she said.

For a moment I was too confused to speak. But as I stared into the woman's eyes, I realized she could not have been Frances. I realized I was looking into eyes that had seen nothing more tragic than a succession of badly decorated bedrooms—rooms in which she had lain alone, with her hands beneath the covers.

My confusion vanished quickly, and I remembered that

Frances had warned me of danger. I welcomed the chance to use my new strength. I smiled and said, "How do you do, Miss Barton. Your first name isn't Frances, is it?"

She looked puzzled. "No," she said. "My name is Anne. But I think it would be more appropriate if you called me Miss Barton. Don't you agree?"

"Oh, yes. I was just being inquisitive, Miss Barton."

The day would come, I was sure, when she would beg me to call her Anne. I would refuse.

On the way down to breakfast we passed her room, where her four unfashionable dresses hung limply in the dark closet, exuding the faint, sour smell of her uninteresting body.

Keith was at school and James had gone out on business. Katherine, Miss Barton, and I sat in the dining room. I ate cold toast and drank bitter tea while they talked nervously, touching each other occasionally, and soon forgetting me. Two neglected women, each already trying to remedy the other's neglect. It seemed unlikely that Miss Barton would be a threat to me.

After breakfast Katherine took Miss Barton on a tour of the house. Katherine knew the age and origin of every carpet, curio, painting, and piece of furniture in the old house. She thought of herself as a historian, but she didn't realize, as Grandmother did, that history is not names and dates, but a gasping young man clutching his stomach with bloodied fingers while another man watches, grinning and holding a marlinespike. There was a marlinespike on the mantel in our dining room. I sometimes took it in my hand and held it tightly until I saw the dying man fall to the deck of the ship. There were other objects in the house that showed me past events. The events were never pleasant. I loved the house, and I hoped I would never have to leave it.

I went to my bedroom, while the women moved through the house, speaking softly, smiling, and running their damp fingertips over walnut paneling, never wondering about those who had gone before them.

Frances was waiting for me in my bedroom.

"Do not underestimate Miss Barton," she said.

"I see no danger."

"You see she has my form."

"Of course. But she doesn't have your strength."

"She is my descendant. My descendants have repudiated me and have denied my power. I tell you again, beware."

I wondered for the first time whether I might have become stronger than Frances.

"I'll be careful," I said. "Rest now."

The image of Frances faded. I went downstairs to the study and waited for Miss Barton to come to me and begin our education. While I waited I picked up a piece of scrimshaw that I had never held before.

At dinner that night James interrupted Grandmother— something I had never heard him do before. The presence of a strange woman in the house had excited him, and I knew he was eager to be with me in the attic.

"Miss Barton," I said, "perhaps you would like me to show you the neighborhood after dinner."

James's flushed face paled slightly. "Wouldn't it be safer to do that in the morning?" he asked.

"But it's so lovely at night."

"Then I'd better come with you," he said.

"Oh, I think they'll be all right," said Katherine. "The muggers stay uptown where there's a wider selection of victims."

James drank some wine.

"Ships once moored outside the door of this house," Grandmother said. "Instead of rumbling trucks, the Cuttners heard the creak of timbers. Ships' bells rang throughout the night."

Miss Barton and I walked through the narrow, deserted streets toward Battery Park. Our faces were pale, faintly reflecting the fluorescent glow of the quiet office buildings, where wastebaskets were being emptied. I wondered whether the night workers were curious about the people who had filled the wastebaskets during the day; whether they found, among the crumpled memos and antacid wrappers, unfinished notes containing passionate words meant to be seen only by one person—or by no one.

I thought of what Grandmother had said. The streets we walked on were once part of the harbor. Landfill had extended the limits of the city; the present had displaced the past.

"Would you rather have lived at another time, Miss Barton?"

"Actually, I would rather not have lived at all. The whole process seems silly to me, but no sillier now than at any other time."

Why would she say such a thing to me? Perhaps she was trying to gain my sympathy.

"Are you surprised that I would admit that to you?" she asked.

"I try not to be surprised."

"I wanted you to know that I intend to answer all of your questions honestly—more honestly than I would answer those of your uncle or aunt. You and I should have a special relationship. I hope you'll be honest with me."

"Yes, of course." I had no intention of being honest with her. I hoped she was not going to take my hand.

We paused at Fraunces Tavern, where George Washington had supposedly delivered his farewell address to his officers in 1783.

"Such a handsome building," Miss Barton said.

I could have told her that it had actually been constructed in 1907 and that a critic had called it "wishful archeology";

that its purpose was to give men like my father a pretentious place to take their clients for lunch. I said nothing.

"There are so few physical reminders of the past in New York," she continued. "I think old objects are so important. They are mirrors in which we can see reflections of former lives."

Was that phrase an accident? Or had I underestimated Miss Barton? I decided it must have been accidental, and I ignored it. We walked through Battery Park. A breeze came in off the water, carrying odors it was best not to try to identify. The park was nearly empty, and the squat bulk of Castle Clinton loomed ahead of us. The castle was an early-nineteenth-century fort, circular and roofless. I didn't know whether men had died there.

We passed the Baby Carriage Woman, a derelict who spent her nights in the park. She pushed an old once-elegant perambulator loaded with things she treasured. There were large bones among her treasures, and she often laughed.

A ferry was leaving for Staten Island, and Miss Barton looked longingly at its lights. I think she was uncomfortable in the darkness. We leaned on the railing at the water's edge, looking out into the harbor. Miss Barton looked to the reassuring figure of the Statue of Liberty, but I thought of my parents and the gray waves of Lake George. James said Mother and Father had not struggled; that they had seemed to welcome the cold, enclosing water. I wondered whether Miss Barton could swim.

We walked back to the house in silence.

Late that night I met James in the attic, and we did things we seldom did—things that caused him pain. I wanted him to cry out so that Miss Barton, who was probably lying awake in the room below us, would hear him and wonder why she had come to live with us.

As James and I left the attic, we paused on the stairway. It was difficult for him to stop touching me. As he held me I looked over his shoulder into the dim light of the hallway below. Suddenly the door to Miss Barton's room opened and James's wife appeared. She moved quickly along the hallway and down the stairs toward her bedroom, glancing up briefly at me with an expression I could not identify. She was barefoot and was wearing a black leather coat.

Six

The next morning at breakfast we smiled often at one another and spoke of inconsequential things. We were much as any other family. We saw the need to conceal the truth of our feelings. We pretended that our appetites could be satisfied with toast and cereal; that our knowledge of evil was limited to what we learned of it from our morning newspaper.

Miss Barton and I began our lessons that morning. They began, as most formal processes do, with deception.

"You are very close to your uncle, aren't you?" she asked.

"I try to be. But I don't think he likes young women. Actually, I think Aunt Katherine is a much warmer person, don't you?"

Miss Barton's face pinkened beneath its layer of heavy, unevenly applied makeup. One wouldn't have thought she spent much time grooming herself. But her bathroom adjoined mine, and that morning I had put my ear to the wall and listened as she tended her body, mumbling and spitting. It had been a remarkably long process, considering the results she achieved. I thought of her resemblance to Frances and of the subtle differences between them. They were both women who were careless of their appearance, but in Frances' case it was the result of indifference. Miss Barton was merely inept.

We were to study European history, English literature, biology, French, and music. I decided I would be a good student, and I didn't expect her to teach me anything meaningful. I knew she wouldn't tell me of Catherine the Great's unnatural fondness for horses or of the Earl of Rochester's celebration of "the happy Minute." I did expect, though, to learn something of the way Frances and her arts were seen by others.

The mirror in the study was round and convex, and as we sat there that morning I could see the distorted face of Frances. She stared constantly at Miss Barton and said once, "Pocky whore." When Frances spoke, Miss Barton, who had been talking about our need to visit a bookstore, paused and looked uneasily about the room. She was to have many such moments.

The household quickly settled into a new routine. Miss Barton and I met in the study each weekday morning from nine o'clock until noon. In the afternoons I was free to read and to prepare assignments. I did very little reading, however, for there was still a great deal I had to learn about the house and the people who shared it with me.

Katherine and Miss Barton were frequently together in the afternoons, and it seemed that each day Katherine's appearance changed in some way. She had previously been a bland, moderate person whose most striking feature was her hair, which was coarse and tightly curled. It was not beautiful hair, but I think some people found it exciting because it so closely resembled pubic hair. I found it repugnant, and I often wished she would cover her head at the table.

She had had her hair cropped short after Miss Barton arrived, making it more ridiculous than ever. She had once had a strangely odorless body, but she began to wear puzzling scents that I eventually decided must be expensive after-shave lotions. Miss Barton often smelled faintly of the same scents.

James had never been happier. He accused Katherine of being in love with Miss Barton and pretended to be outraged. Actually, the thought of his wife being involved with another woman excited him, and the real and pretended emotions of the situation enriched his life. He became much more open about his relationship with me, and on afternoons when Katherine and Miss Barton were uptown shopping together he would take me to his wife's bed. "You be Katherine," he'd say, "and I'll be Miss Barton."

Occasionally there was an afternoon when everyone but Grandmother was out of the house. On those days I would visit rooms.

Those visits were among my greatest pleasures. I think everyone must feel excitement at being alone in a room where someone else lives. It is the excitement one feels even in a motel room. No matter how neat and impersonal the room, it is permeated with the private acts of those who were there before. The pleasure of being in a room that contains the objects of another's life is, for me, almost overpowering.

Frances followed me on my visits. As I carefully opened drawers she watched me from the always-present mirrors. Under Miss Barton's carefully folded underwear there were three picture books and a package of long, curved needles.

In Keith's room his snakes lay coiled among rocks in glass tanks. In a corner was a cage in which mice skittered and sniffed, each awaiting the moment when it would find itself desperately trying to climb the glass walls of a snake tank as lean, cold bodies uncoiled.

I spent a few moments in the Taylors' room. Their closet

contained more shoes than one would have expected to find; some of them would fit only a child.

Seven

Miss Barton and I were in the study. The walnut shutters were open, and the morning sun cast a bright, gradually changing rectangle on the old Turkish carpet. I often stared at the carpet's intricate design as Miss Barton murmured her informal lectures. Occasionally she would seem to forget what she was saying, and I would glance up to find her staring at me in a sort of gentle confusion. It was difficult to believe that she had anything but admiration for me.

"Where did you live in England, Miss Barton?"

She smiled, and the look of confusion vanished. It was the first time I had asked her a personal question since we had walked together in the park.

"I was born in Chelmsford. Do you know where that is?"

"No."

"It's in the County of Essex, just north of London. Bartons have lived there for at least four hundred years."

I remembered Grandmother having mentioned Essex. "Does it have an interesting history?"

"No. Not particularly. Probably the only noteworthy events were the witchcraft trials of the sixteenth and seventeenth centuries. I'm told that at least one of my ancestors was accused of witchcraft."

"You don't believe in the supernatural, do you?"

The early-autumn sun was behind Miss Barton, backlighting the heavy fuzz on her cheeks and concealing her expression. "I don't think it can be easily dismissed," she said. "A great many people have believed themselves bewitched, and many have confessed to being witches even when their confessions might result in death. Anything that people believe that intensely must be taken seriously."

Frances had appeared in the convex mirror. She usually found my tutoring sessions dull, and would appear only indistinctly, staring at Miss Barton but seldom speaking.

"Show her your mark," Frances said to me.

I moved my chair so that the lower part of my body was in the sun, and I slowly crossed my legs, allowing my skirt to ride up as if by accident. Miss Barton knew, as all women know, that such things are never accidental. I yawned slowly, closing my eyes and then opening them quickly. Miss Barton was staring at my thighs and biting her lower lip. My mark was brilliant in the sunlight.

Miss Barton spoke my name, her deep-shadowed face revealing what might have been either fear or desire. Frances laughed.

There was a knock on the door, and James entered the room. He often visited us in the morning before he left to go uptown, supposedly for business meetings.

I think Miss Barton was frightened of James. I don't know why that should have been, for he was no more complex or evil than his young son. He often pretended to flirt with her and then smiled at her discomfort.

"Hello, ladies. Is there anything I can bring you from uptown? Perhaps a longer skirt for you, Elizabeth."

He was jealous.

"Do you think I'm old enough for that?" I asked.

"We're never too young to learn modesty, are we, Miss Barton?" he said.

Miss Barton frowned, perhaps in anger. "I think I prefer innocence to modesty," she said.

"We all do," he said. "But innocence can't be learned, can it?"

"Perhaps not," said Miss Barton. "It isn't a subject I teach, in any case."

She was beginning to relax. She disliked James, but she found his question distracting. It was something I had soon discovered about her. When she was short-tempered with me, I had only to ask her something about a subject that interested her, and she soon became absorbed in her answer, or more precisely, in herself. I have learned that the things people say are irrelevant to their true nature. If I had known Miss Barton only by her words, I might have thought she was virtuous; that she wished me well.

"Can evil be learned?" I asked.

Frances smiled.

Dinners became awkward after Miss Barton came to live with us. Grandmother was interested in learning what Miss Barton knew about our family history, but she could not alter her habit of never addressing anyone individually at the table.

A system was quickly worked out. Grandmother would introduce the subject she wanted to learn about, and Miss Barton would then tell the rest of us what she knew about the subject. They spoke of the Cuttners as well as of the Bartons. Miss Barton was less interesting than Grandmother, probably out of a misguided concern for Keith's sensibilities.

One night Grandmother said, "In 1592 Frances Barton, who lived in Hatfield Peverel, near Chelmsford, was accused of witchcraft."

We were eating lamb chops, which Mrs. Taylor had undercooked. Our plates were bright with blood. We waited for Miss Barton to speak.

"Frances Barton had long been suspected of witchcraft," she said after hesitating and glancing at me. "At her trial her body was examined, and a red mark was found on her chest. She admitted having drawn a circle on the ground in front of a neighbor's house. The neighbor woman had found a toad within the circle, and shortly afterward her child had drowned. Frances was convicted and died of a fever in prison."

When Miss Barton mentioned the witch's mark, James, who had been drawing his knife through the red meat on his plate, paused and raised his eyes to mine.

I winked at him.

That night I found a snake on my bed.

I had gone to my room to practice my music. Miss Barton was teaching me to play the flute, and two or three nights a week I would spend an hour making decidedly unmusical sounds on the instrument. I have never seen the point of music, and as I tried to practice, my mind was always occupied with images and thoughts of other, more meaningful things. Nevertheless, I did learn to play one melody reasonably well. It was a tune that Frances taught me. It was in a minor key, and when I first played it for Miss Barton, she pretended to admire it, but I saw the skin on her forearms contract into tiny bumps.

I had left my flute on my bed, and when I entered my room that night the bright shaft of the instrument was encircled by a dark band that I thought at first was a length of heavy black ribbon. But then I saw that the ribbon was slowly moving, sinuously entwining itself around the flute. As I moved closer I could see the hard muscles beneath the scaly, glittering skin. The snake continued its slow, spiraling motion, and I thought Keith must have put it there, either to frighten me or as a gift.

Then I heard Frances speak: "It's time you had a new imp, my pet."

I turned to the mirror. Frances was looking at me tenderly. There was gray in her hair, and her face was flushed. I was seeing her as she must have appeared in her final days of imprisonment. I realized that the resemblance between her and Miss Barton was superficial. Their eyes had looked on different things in profoundly different ways. My important lessons were being learned not from the self-engrossed, bland Miss Barton, but from Frances, who existed only for me.

"Touch him, Elizabeth."

I sat on the bed and reached out to the snake. I touched its triangular head and ran my fingers slowly along its cool, hard body. It began to move up my arm, finally encircling my neck and pushing its head into the front of my blouse, seeking the warmth of my body.

I called the snake Imp, and it shared my bed each night.

Eight

I believe I am a lovable person. I don't know why that should be, for I have neither given love nor sought it. But I do not reject it when it is offered to me by those who pretend to understand and need it. I think perhaps love is evil. Certainly a great many evil acts have been performed under its influence. Miss Barton spoke of love with great respect and often pointed out its effect on history and literature, but I was not interested in her romantic theories. I was more impressed by the fact that Anne Boleyn had six fingers on one of her hands than I was by Henry's professed love for her.

James was not the only one who loved me or to whom I brought happiness.

I became Keith's only friend. I let him speak to me of snakes, and when he asked me, I showed him things he had only read about or had heard described in confusing whispers by other boys at school. He did not say so, but Keith loved me.

Katherine had been a distraught person before I became

her daughter. She had sought stability by trying to become a part of the house and its furnishings; she quietly climbed the circular staircase, walked the corridors, winding intricate old clocks, taking mementos in her trembling fingers, curious, confused. I brought Miss Barton to her, relieving her of the obligation to serve James's alien needs. Katherine's love for me was as neurotically simple as her other emotions.

Miss Barton wanted to change me, but being a teacher, she didn't know how. And being a rational person, she didn't know why. She loved me and she thought, therefore, that she could bring me only good. I'm sure that most people would have found Miss Barton modest, intelligent, and admirable in almost every way. But I knew she had an instrument with which she removed the blackheads from Katherine's ears.

Not everyone would have admired James. Some would have found his body too carefully cared for and his mind too much in disarray. He would rightfully have been suspected of being the kind of man who would dance naked and grinning as his adopted daughter played a strange melody on the flute.

And so we formed a community joined in happiness. The others thought our happiness sprang from love. Only I knew we were controlled by another force—one that only I could see. I hoped it would never change. I knew there would be threats to our happiness, and I was prepared to resist them through any means.

One of the threats began when Grandmother received a visitor. It had been years since she had seen anyone except those who lived in the house. Her social life had ended with her divorce, and James protected her from people who wanted to see her about business.

On the afternoon of the visit I had gone uptown to the main branch of the public library on Forty-second Street. I seldom left the house, and when I did, I almost never went north of Canal Street and Chinatown. Most often I walked past the neglected docks, where I could smell the foul, complex odors and look into the dark water, where pale half-submerged objects moved in the currents.

I was uncomfortable in midtown Manhattan, where the rivers seemed so distant and where the new buildings stood as featureless as tombstones. No one else seemed to notice the hovering, screaming gulls that drifted far above us. And no one else seemed to recognize any of his or her own qualities in the derelicts who sprawled or limped in the park behind the library.

Once in the library, moving past the guards and through the turnstile, I relaxed. It was a building in which there were things to look at: carved wood, rich-patterned marble, gilded ceilings, silly murals. In the main reading room I found two books in which Frances was mentioned. The Assize indictments of 1590 recorded that Frances Barton was an enchantress, and that she was accused of consorting with a "cunning man" who located missing objects. The disposition of the case was not indicated. In 1592 she was listed as a woman of filthy behavior and accused and convicted of bewitching a child to death.

I closed the books and looked about the enormous reading room. There were scores of people at the heavy oak tables: people seeking information, entertainment, or refuge. You would not have said they were people who controlled things. They looked powerless, as Frances did in her time and as I did now. Yet Frances was made to suffer because of her powers, and I knew that someday I too might have to face the judgment of the resentful or the envious.

As I was about to enter the house that afternoon a man stood in the doorway of the adjoining building.

"Elizabeth?" he said.

"Yes."

"I am your grandfather."

"Mr. Cuttner?"

"James told me you were living with him. I wondered whether you would like to see my offices and get to know me."

I didn't answer him. I was curious about what kind of man he was, but it would have seemed disloyal to Grandmother if I were to become friendly with him.

"Why don't you come in now if you have a few minutes," he said.

"I couldn't stay long."

"I wouldn't expect you to. I wouldn't expect anything except some curiosity or perhaps some apprehension."

He opened the door and stood aside. He had the same kind of charming manner my father had cultivated, a charm that people found discomforting because it was based on weakness. I walked through the doorway. It was after five o'clock, and there was no sign of the other people who worked there.

The door closed behind me, and in the silence of the building I heard Mr. Cuttner's lips separate; the tiny sound of mucous membranes pulling apart. He breathed through his mouth, closing it occasionally to swallow and to moisten his lips. I wondered how Grandmother had been able to live with him.

"It's not as handsome a building as yours," he said. "We've had to make some allowances for commerce. And for my health."

There was an elevator door ahead of me. But it matched the polished wood paneling of the foyer. Framed engravings and photographs of ships crowded the walls.

Mr. Cuttner's office was on the second floor, separated by a few inches of brick and plaster from Grandmother's room in the adjoining building. We sat and spoke of my parents' death and of my life with James. I avoided the truth, and he was pleased. He told me of his business, which was his life, and I wondered what truths he was avoiding.

As he spoke I picked up a letter opener from his desk. I held its whale-tooth handle tightly, and I saw superimposed over Mr. Cuttner's face a faint image of Grandmother. She was standing naked in the arms of a man. It was not the Grandmother I now knew, but a younger woman. Her hair had not yet whitened, and her eyes were those of a person who saw the present rather than the past. I did not recognize the man who held her, but I knew it was someone I had seen before.

I put the letter opener down, and Grandfather came back into sharp focus again.

"I hope we'll be friends," he was saying. "And I want you to drop in whenever you like."

As I left I realized I had seen no mirrors in the building.

Grandmother's chair was empty at the dinner table that night. She was in her room with a visitor, James told us. We dined in silence, each of us resenting the change in our routine and wondering who could have persuaded Grandmother to change her habits even for one night. I think the others realized for the first time how important a part Grandmother played in their lives. She sustained them not only with her house and her money, but also with her aloof presence and her sense of family history. But she had not supplied moral authority; that was to be supplied by Frances, through me.

From time to time the others glanced uneasily at Grandmother's empty chair. I ignored the chair and noticed instead how they invariably turned their eyes to me after looking at her vacant place. I realized that in her absence, my place became the head of the table.

I think Miss Barton was the first to understand what was happening. She began to speak of the past, hoping to take on some of Grandmother's authority. She stopped her monologue when Keith began to giggle and Katherine blushed. The room became silent again except for the small, unpleasant sounds of food being consumed.

I went to my room after dinner, and Frances was waiting for me.

"James will not visit you this evening," she said.

There were nights when she prevented him from seeing me, nights when she and I were to be alone together. I changed into my nightgown and sat before the mirror. The house was exceptionally still, and I thought I could hear the faint throb of engines as a ship moved through the darkness of the harbor.

"There is a stranger in the house," said Frances.

"Yes. Have you seen him?"

"Aye. He speaks of death."

"May I see him?"

"I cannot conjure him for you. But be upon the stairway at midnight, when he leaves her."

I began to comb my hair, playing a game with Frances that we both found exciting. As the comb moved rhythmically and slowly through my hair, our images began to alternate in the mirror. Static crackled around the comb, and I hummed the melody Frances had taught me. I thought about how real she had become to me and how her presence comforted me. I knew that whatever problems might arise, she would help me overcome them, and that as long as we were together we would prevail.

Just before midnight I went to the staircase and sat in the shadows, where I could see the door to Grandmother's room. In a few minutes the door opened and a man's figure appeared. His back was to me and I saw him only in silhouette, yet there was something familiar about him. Then I remembered what I had seen in Mr. Cuttner's office earlier. The man before me was the same man I had seen embracing Grandmother. The door closed quickly, and the man turned to leave. It was Mr. Hurlbut, the caretaker of our cabin at Lake George.

He had spoken of death, Frances said. I remembered his expression as he and James had stood before me at the lake that morning. I hadn't known then what lay behind his expression. Now I knew: it was unwanted knowledge.

He quickly vanished down the stairs, leaving behind him the harsh odor of a man unconcerned with the opinions of those who lived in heated rooms.

Nine

At the breakfast table the next morning we tried to pretend that the danger had passed. Katherine and Miss Barton played their obvious, pathetic games.

"More coffee, Katherine?" Miss Barton went to the sideboard and brought back the large silver pot. She pressed her heavy thigh against Katherine's shoulder as she stood beside her and refilled her cup.

James smiled faintly as he watched them. "Is there some there for me, Anne?" he asked.

Miss Barton went to his side, and as she poured, he ran his hand delicately across the back of her tight, wrinkled skirt. Her hands began to tremble, and coffee spilled into his saucer.

It was James's nature to want to complicate relationships, and I knew it was inevitable that he would try to bring Miss Barton under his influence. He lacked the intelligence or subtlety to influence even her commonplace mind, and he had no choice except to approach her physically.

I wondered whether James was a dangerous person. He

had always seemed harmless enough to me, but perhaps that was because we shared certain desires. What would it have been like if I stood between him and his desires? I remembered the broken screen door.

I was the first one to see Grandmother. She was standing in the doorway of the dining room, looking at us with an expression I had never seen on her face before. It was possibly not as simple as anger, but it was a look of judgment and disapproval. She was wearing a white blouse, a gray tweed skirt, a red cardigan sweater, and a long string of gray baroque pearls.

After Miss Barton was seated, Grandmother moved to her usual place at the head of the table. "I remind you that you are all here at my sufferance," she said. "I'm sure you realize that. And I remind you that you are all children of one sort or another; I hope you realize that. Does anyone deny it?"

It occurred to me that Grandmother might have gone insane, and I wondered what Mr. Hurlbut had done or said to her on the previous night. No one seemed inclined to answer her question. Katherine and Miss Barton stared at their plates as though they were indeed children, and James grinned in fascination and shock.

"I am not a child, Mrs. Cuttner," I said.

"It doesn't follow, Elizabeth, that because you are old enough to be evil, you are an adult."

"Now really, Mother," said James. "I think your visitor has upset you. Perhaps we can talk at dinner. Why don't you rest this morning?"

I knew what had to be done. I got up and went to Grandmother. I took her hand in mine and said, "Yes, Grandmother. I'll take you to your room. We can talk later."

She looked down at my hand. She was growing confused. "Evil," she said. "Frances is guilty. Frances must be revealed." She looked at the morning light on her red sweater, and she began to weep.

James was behind her. The pleasure he had been taking in the situation had apparently turned to fear. "Come along with us," he said. We led her to her room as she wept quietly.

Heavy drapes were hung over the shuttered windows, and the room was lighted by a flickering gaslight fixture on the wall. Most of the rooms in the house had such fixtures, but I had not realized they still operated. I could not make out many details in the clutter of the darkened room, but above a massive dresser was a large oval mirror with a carved wood frame. Frances was watching us.

Grandmother took her hand from mine and sat on the bed. Her sobbing had stopped.

"Leave us, Elizabeth," she said. "Your uncle and I must talk."

Now that we were no longer touching, I could see her strength returning. I didn't want to leave her alone with James, but he said to me, "It will be all right. Leave us."

As I left the musty dimness of the room, I looked back. Grandmother once again looked confident and strong, as she had when she entered the dining room. James was seated in an enormous leather wing chair. He looked small and weak, and I knew that whatever they were to discuss, Grandmother would prevail. She did not fear his touch.

I went to my room and closed the shutters. I reached for the gaslight fixture and twisted the valve. It gradually began to turn, and I heard a faint hiss. I found some matches that James had left on the dresser, and I lighted the gas. It was obvious why Grandmother preferred the soft, flickering light to electric bulbs. How pleasant it would have been to sit in her room and listen to her speaking of the past, to examine objects that were concealed in dark corners.

That was not possible now. She had been corrupted, and soon the light would fill her room, destroying the world that had been created by darkness and her presence.

"We must act," said Frances. "I shall instruct you tonight."

Miss Barton was waiting for me in the study. She was seated stiffly in a straight-backed chair. She was trying to forget that I had taught her to sit cross-legged on the floor, to remove her shoes, to laugh, and sometimes to be careless with her skirt.

"Did you speak to your grandmother?"

"No. James is talking to her."

"I hope she's not ill. A sudden change in personality is seldom a good sign."

"Change is inevitable, isn't it, Miss Barton? Haven't you changed since you've been with us?"

"Not in any fundamental way. I've made new friends, and I've had to adjust to them, that's all. In any case, it's my job to change you, not to be changed."

"Have you succeeded in your job?"

"How do you mean?"

"Have you changed me?"

"No, Elizabeth, not yet. But I think I shall succeed eventually—when you want me to."

I believe Miss Barton thought of herself as a virtuous person. Perhaps she thought virtue lay in what she believed rather than in what she was.

James entered the study. I had always thought James knew exactly what he was and that he accepted his nature without question. But at that moment he looked as though he might have some sort of regrets. If someone had suddenly thrown something at him, he would not have raised his arms.

"Mother wants to send you to a boarding school, Elizabeth. Immediately. And, Anne, you would have to leave us."

"How extraordinary," said Miss Barton. "Did she say why she wants that arrangement?"

"Not really. She talks vaguely of evil, but I don't know what she means by it."

I wondered if James was telling the truth.

"Do we have to do what she says?" asked Miss Barton.

"I suppose we do. It's her house, and she decides who lives in it."

"Why don't we go somewhere else to live?" I asked, knowing that James would find that inconceivable. He would have had to go back into business and smile at men he didn't like.

"I don't think that will be necessary," he said. "I think we can talk her out of this nonsense. Just as someone must have talked her into it."

"Who is Frances?" asked Miss Barton. "She said Frances is guilty."

"It's someone she imagines," said James. "She'll forget it, and I think we should too."

James was powerless. He supposed, as most people do, that if he waited and hoped, things would be as he wanted them to be. There are other methods.

Grandmother did not appear for dinner that night. Mr. Taylor said she asked to have some food sent to her room. Mrs. Taylor had apparently been affected by the change in the household routine. She prepared sweetbreads, rubbery and glandular, in a bland sauce. Keith ran from the table, gagging. James drank too much wine, Miss Barton's hands trembled, and Katherine's foot touched mine under the table.

After dinner I went to my room. I opened the box in which I kept Imp, my snake. I reached out to him, and he quickly wrapped his black, glistening body around my forearm. I went to the mirror, where Frances awaited me.

"Grandmother says you are guilty," I said.

"She knows naught of me."

"She wants me to leave this house."

"You shan't leave. Heed me. Nearby there is a circular structure. Go there anon with Imp and a small glass. You will know what to do. Rest now."

As Frances' image faded I began to feel exhausted and drowsy. I went to the bed and stretched out, unsure of what lay ahead of me, but certain that this would be the most extraordinary night I had ever experienced. Within a few minutes I was asleep.

I was awakened by an inexplicable sound. It was very close to me, and as I slowly opened my eyes, I saw a figure leaving the room. It was Miss Barton, and she held a pair of scissors in her hand. When I saw the scissors I realized that what I had heard was the sound of hair being cut. I looked down at my shoulder, where a length of my hair rested. At one point its ends were notched unevenly, and a few loose clippings had fallen on my blouse. Why would Miss Barton take a lock of my hair? I was about to go after her when I remembered that there was something more important for me to do. I got ready to leave the house.

The night was clear and cool. A full moon was rising over the harbor, its cold luminescence contrasting with the scattered yellow lights of passing ships and distant shore lights. The squat, thick walls of Castle Clinton loomed ahead of me. Once the building had been separated from the mainland, impregnable and threatening. Now, joined to Manhattan by landfill, it was dwarfed by a semicircle of glowing office buildings. I wasn't sure that I could enter the old fortress as Frances had instructed me. Normally the heavy doors were padlocked at night, but I found only a heavy bolt that slid open slowly as I leaned my weight against it.

Inside the fortress, with the door closed, I rested for a moment. The city's presence had vanished except for the glow it cast in the sky above the roofless walls. Gravel scraped beneath my feet as I moved to the center of the circular yard. I felt Imp stir in the canvas bag I carried. I released him, and he skittered ahead of me, dark against the light gravel. He coiled himself precisely in the center of the area.

Moving toward the snake, I took a small round hand mirror from the bag and placed it on the nestlike coil of Imp's body.

"Martha," I found myself saying, "with my gift and power I bid thee desist. Martha Cuttner, I bid thee vanish. Thrice. Martha Cuttner, my gift and power bid thee desist and vanish."

And then there was silence. Behind me stood the city and its people. Some of those people had passed me on the street and admired me, thinking I had never done unmentionable things in the night, as they had done or had wanted to do.

The moon was beginning to show over the wall of the fortress, and I stared at it, oblivious of everything else, until it was fully visible. As its last brilliant edge cleared the wall, there was a shattering sound at my feet, and I looked down to see that the mirror had broken and Imp had vanished. When I raised my head again a dense cloud was moving across the moon. I began to tremble, and then I was running through the quiet streets, feeling an elation that some might have confused with terror.

No lights could be seen in the buildings along Coenties Slip. The short street was empty except for James's car, which was parked in front of our house. I paused at the corner, wondering what had happened while I was gone. There was nothing unusual to see or hear from where I stood, but as I approached our doorway I heard a faint creaking sound. I stopped again. The sound was not coming from our house, but from next door in the offices of Mr. Cuttner. In a second-floor window there was a pale, vague-featured shape that could have been a face—a face that had seen something intolerable.

As I entered my room I heard the sound of splashing water. The bathroom door was ajar, releasing a bar of light across the floor of the darkened bedroom, where James's clothes were scattered. I called to him, and in a moment he was pressing his wet body against me and singing to me in Italian. I think it was an aria from Mozart's *Don Giovanni*. When he stopped singing, he whispered, "Leave your clothes on." He was happy again.

Ten

"I'll be distressed if I have to leave you," Miss Barton said. "But I suppose it would be good for you to return to school, to be among young people again."

We were in the study, about to begin a class in poetry. There had been no mention of Grandmother at breakfast. The others had seemed apprehensive at first, as though they were expecting the old woman to appear and threaten their happiness as she had the previous morning. But I had reassured them. I spoke of future pleasures, and they soon began to smile, becoming absorbed in selfish fantasies.

And now, when we were supposed to be talking about poetry, Miss Barton was still absorbed in her fantasy.

"Do you miss being with people your own age?" she asked.

She wanted me to tell her that I found her vastly more interesting than I had ever found anyone of my own age. I wouldn't give her that kind of satisfaction, though.

"I miss some of them," I said. "I often think of Miranda."

"Miranda? I don't remember your mentioning her before."

"We were very close for a time. But she became a woman before I did, and I didn't always understand some of the things she wanted me to do."

Miss Barton raised her eyebrows slightly. "What sort of things?"

"Personal things. She once asked me to give her a lock of my hair."

"Surely there's nothing wrong with that," Miss Barton said. Her eyebrows had lowered and she seemed embarrassed.

"Not in itself, I suppose. But there was definitely something wrong with what she wanted to do with the hair."

Miss Barton didn't ask me what that might have been. I'm not sure what I would have told her if she had asked. She stared at me, probably wondering whether I had seen her leaving my room the previous night.

When I thought she had wondered long enough, I said, "Shall we read some poetry?"

I enjoyed the system we had for studying poems. Miss Barton would read a poem aloud, and then we would discuss what she had read. She chose poems from all periods, and did not tell me who the author was until after we had discussed the poem. I thought it remarkable how similar most poems were to one another even when they had been written centuries apart. Perhaps it was because the behavior of the insane varies little from century to century.

"Are most poets mad?" I asked.

Miss Barton looked pleased. I think I was the first person she had tutored who liked poetry. "It's possible," she answered. "At least most of them have been unusual. That's why we value them."

"Do you think I'm an unusual person?"

Miss Barton looked at me seriously. "Yes," she said. "But

not as unusual as you might think. Everyone is strange in some way."

"Then you are strange too."

"Yes." She touched my hand. "But not in a way that harms anyone. It's important that you not harm anyone, Elizabeth."

Like most powerless persons, Miss Barton made a virtue of her weakness. I took her hand and said, "I wouldn't try to harm anyone who loved me."

When Grandmother didn't appear for dinner that night, James asked Mr. Taylor to see if she wanted some dinner sent to her room. I think Mr. Taylor was devoted to Grandmother. He had served tea for her on afternoons long ago when her hand, as she reached for her cup, was smooth and unveined. He had polished her shoes, placing his large hand into the dark pocket of still-damp leather, his eyes closed, smiling.

He was not smiling when he returned to the dining room that night. He leaned over and whispered hesitantly to James.

James looked at me. "Has anyone seen Mother? She's not in her room."

No one answered.

James said to Mr. Taylor, "She can't have gone out. We'd better have a look around the house."

"I'll help," I said. I wanted to see Grandmother's room again.

The fragments of the mirror were strewn across the floor and the top of the dresser, reflecting the gentle flame of the gaslight. James and Mr. Taylor looked at the scattered fragments and were silent. I think the broken mirror frightened them more than Grandmother's absence; it was an omen. They had been taught that it would bring bad luck, but they knew it was more than that. They knew that there had been life in the glass; that the thousands of images that constituted the history of that room had disintegrated with the mirror. A life had been destroyed.

James pushed a wall switch, and the room was filled with a brilliant light. Suspended from the high ceiling was a small but elaborate cut-glass chandelier which concealed several powerful bulbs. The walls and ceiling were flecked with dazzling reflections from the glass of the mirror and chandelier. The room, which had previously seemed exciting and mysterious, now seemed only pathetic and neglected.

We gathered in the study after searching the house. Grandmother could not be found, of course, and no one found anything that indicated what might have become of her.

Although I knew I was responsible for the disappearance, I don't believe I felt any guilt. I had only been an intermediary between her meddlesome nature and other forces. I had not taken a weapon to her; I had not pushed my thumbs against her windpipe or held her head beneath water. She had simply vanished, and it had been the result of her own actions.

James stood before the fireplace. "There's no evidence of any violence or struggle, except for the broken mirror," he said. "I don't think there's any need to be alarmed as yet."

Katherine, who was sitting stiffly on a sofa with her arm around Keith, asked, "When was she last seen?"

"Mr. Taylor took some dinner to her room last night. He collected her tray about nine o'clock. Did anyone see her after that?"

No one replied.

"It's possible she went out somewhere," said Katherine.

"What about her visitor?" asked Miss Barton. "Does anyone know who it was or when he left?"

"Taylor let him in," said James, "but it was no one he recognized. The man gave him a note to take to Mother, and she said she would see him in her room. I don't know when he left, but Taylor said he was still there at nine o'clock."

They wanted to make a mystery of the disappearance —not the splendid kind of mystery it actually was, but the kind they watched on television programs. I wouldn't tell them I had seen Mr. Hurlbut. Whatever he had shared with Grandmother on that night should be his secret. We are all entitled to secrets. Could we face the world comfortably without some unshared knowledge? Knowledge of what had taken place with another in a darkened room?

"Where might she have gone?" asked Katherine.

"It's been years since she left the house. Not since she used to go to Lake George."

"I suppose it's conceivable that she went there," said James. "She used to go there on impulse fairly often."

I wished they wouldn't pretend to be concerned. They were ashamed to admit their relief.

James was especially excited. He constantly ran his small, pointed tongue across his dry lips. "There's nothing more we can do tonight. If she's not back by morning, maybe I'll drive up to the lake. If I don't find her there, we can notify someone. I don't think we can do anything else for now."

Keith went to his room, and the rest of us sat without speaking. The house was silent, but outside a heavy rain had begun to fall.

Miss Barton moved to the sofa, next to Katherine. James poured cognac for us. "To my ladies," he said.

On my way upstairs I went into Grandmother's room. I switched off the lights of the chandelier and slowly turned the control on the gaslight until the room was in darkness.

I left and closed the door, depriving the shattered mirror of the last vestiges of light.

When I reached my room I expected Frances to be waiting for me, but she did not appear. I sat before the mirror and called to her, but I saw only my own face. There was a fine line across my forehead, a line I had never seen before. And I was feeling something I had never felt before: the fear that I might never again see someone whom I valued.

Eleven

James left for Lake George in his small red car early the next morning. I had expected him to ask me to go with him. He found it exciting to be with me in an automobile, and sometimes he would let me drive. "Faster, faster," he would whisper, smiling as the car swerved repeatedly into the gravel at the side of the road. I believe he was indifferent to death.

I was the only one who wanted to be in the house that morning. After Keith left for school, Katherine asked Miss Barton and me to go uptown with her. She was going shopping for clothes. It pleased her to visit small stores off Fifth Avenue; to draw the dressing-room curtain; to remove her dress and replace it with one that had perhaps been tried on by another wealthy, ungainly woman. It pleased her to have the saleswoman stand with her before the full-length mirror, touch her breasts, and say, "It is very good for you here, madame."

We refused the invitation, but after Katherine left, Miss Barton said we should get some fresh air. We walked toward Battery Park. I disliked the narrow streets in the daytime, their character lost in crowds and harsh light. As we entered the park I became aware of the sky. The Battery is one of the few places in Manhattan where more than a narrow wedge of sky is visible. The storm of the previous night was clearing, and low, dark clouds were being driven quickly before a strong wind. For a moment the pink and beige sandstone of Castle Clinton reflected a brilliant patch of sunlight, and then was washed in the gray shadows of a cloud.

"I've never been on the Staten Island ferry," Miss Barton said. "Is it a long ride?"

"The round trip takes about an hour."

"Would you come with me now?"

I would have preferred to return to the house. I wanted to be alone in Grandmother's room, to look in her closets, to touch old objects. Miss Barton would not have left me alone in any case, though, so I agreed to make the boat trip with her.

The ferry was not ready for boarding, and we wandered through the waiting room. I think people tend to reveal their true natures in such places, when sharing boredom with strangers. The older people sat dead-eyed, regretting the past or fearing the future. Children ran and screamed, engrossed in their movements, understanding nothing.

Despite the strong, chilling wind, we stood at the stern of the ship for a few minutes as we moved away from shore. I tried to locate our house, but that was impossible. No one would have suspected its existence among the tightly packed towers that surrounded it. Yet I thought the Cuttner house might be remembered long after its neighboring buildings, with their desks and computers, had been forgotten.

We went into the sheltered main area of the ship and sat on a wooden bench next to a grimy window. We were passing the Statue of Liberty, and Miss Barton pretended to admire it. I knew she was pretending, because we had talked about art many times and she seemed to have a particular understanding of sculpture.

I said, "I think its size is the only impressive thing about it. If it were small enough to fit in the corner of your room, don't you think you might find it silly?"

She smiled. "Perhaps," she said. "It is mostly drapery, isn't it?"

"And a funny hat."

"Nevertheless, I'm moved by it," she said. "I suppose I'm affected by its symbolism. It meant so much to the people who came here from Europe in the nineteenth century—including relatives of mine."

I pointed out Ellis Island, abandoned now, dark and low in the water like an old ship, its elaborate buildings sheltering rats and beetles. "I feel that way about the island," I said. "The first time I saw it I thought I could hear voices across the water—frightened voices."

Miss Barton shivered and looked away from the window. The shoeshine man moved past us. He was a small man who always dressed in black and carried a black box with a footrest on top and a stool attached to it. He never looked up or spoke, staring always at the deck and at the feet of passengers.

"Will you shine my shoes?" I asked him.

He stopped in front of me and squatted on the stool. He began to remove my right shoe.

"No," I said. "I'll keep them on."

I placed my right foot on the slippery metal footrest. The man dipped his right hand into a can of polish and then began to rub his fingertips over my shoe. The polish felt cool through the thin leather. If the man had raised his eyes, he would have seen the red mark on my thigh, but he looked only at my feet. Miss Barton had forgotten the harbor.

When the man had gone, I asked Miss Barton if she was going to miss Grandmother.

"You speak as if you knew she won't return," she said.

"She won't."

The flush that had risen in her face began to pale. "You know where she is, then?"

"No."

"Then you can't be sure, can you? You're just imagining you know something."

I remembered that James had once said Miss Barton was an imaginative person. I had seen little evidence of it. She had learned of exceptional people but she understood only the ordinary. Her mind was a catalog and her emotions were no more refined or controlled than those of the cats that appeared on our streets at night.

"Don't you believe imagining is a way of knowing?" I asked.

She gave me a teacherly look, my feet forgotten. "There's a difference between imagining and imagination. It's important that you know that," she said.

I realized that her world was one of words. Mine was one of knowledge and power.

On the return trip we met Mr. Cuttner. We were standing at the bow of the ferry, watching the bulky ship maneuver into its berth, when we heard his harsh voice behind us.

"Hello, Elizabeth."

I wanted to ignore him, but he moved in front of me. As I looked at him I heard the moaning sound the ship made as it scraped against pilings.

"I wish I'd known you were aboard," he said. "I'd have taken you up to the bridge with me. I've been talking to the captain."

I introduced him to Miss Barton. He took her hand and at the same time put his arm around my shoulder. I knew he was probably a lonely man, but he had no right to inflict his loneliness on me. I remembered that James had said the mention of Grandmother invariably upset Grandfather.

"Grandmother has disappeared," I said. "You haven't seen her, have you?"

He lowered his arms and stepped back from us. He was no longer smiling, and his lower lip was slack. But I doubted whether he was as disturbed as he seemed.

"It's been some years since I've seen your grandmother," he said.

I wondered whether he still loved her or whether he had ever loved her. As I stared at him, the landing ramps were being lowered and the people around us began to leave the ship. I moved forward, wanting to be free of the old man and his emotions. I wanted to think of the shoeshine man, alone now, his pockets heavy with coins, awaiting his next faceless customers.

Mr. Cuttner walked to the house with us, asking questions about Grandmother and trying his best to charm Miss Barton. Even though his ability to charm and hers to be charmed were feeble, they seemed to like each other. He said he might drop in after dinner. It hadn't occurred to me that with Grandmother gone, he might want to reclaim his family. I didn't see any room for him in our household, and I wondered how James would react to the old man's presence.

James telephoned from the lake that afternoon. He said he had found no trace of Grandmother, and he was going to stay overnight at the cabin.

Mr. Taylor was the only man in our house that night. I gave him instructions to admit no callers, and when he said he thought he should ask Katherine about it, I assured him that was not necessary. And I asked him if he could come to my room after dinner and fix a dresser drawer that had been sticking. I had expected him to say it might be more convenient for him to look at it in the morning during my lessons, but instead he looked at me solemnly and agreed.

Katherine wore a new dress at dinner. It was a color that

people shouldn't have to look at while they were eating, and it had short sleeves that were squeezing red circles around the pale flesh of her upper arms.

I was wearing black.

After dinner I went to my room and sat for a few minutes, hoping Frances would appear. When I realized I would not be seeing her, I went to the dresser and pulled out the drawer I kept my underwear in. I took out a pair of black panties and put them in the space between the drawer and the side of the dresser. I pushed the drawer in until it jammed. Then I picked up my flute and practiced until I heard a gentle knock on the door.

Mr. Taylor had brought a toolbox with him. Leaving the bedroom door open, he went to the dresser and put the box on the floor. I showed him which drawer was stuck, and I stood close to him as he carefully pulled at it. It sprang open immediately, and he removed it, reaching in and lifting out the panties. I had expected him to blush, but he said calmly, "I remember you when you were an infant, Elizabeth. I was an old man even then."

He opened the toolbox and looked at the neatly arranged, meticulously clean tools, which smelled faintly of oil. It was the first time I had seen a look of fondness on his face. He found a stick of waxlike lubricant, which he rubbed on the runners of the drawer.

"It should be all right now," he said.

"What was I like as a child?" I asked him.

"I believe you often did unwelcome things."

"Was I naughty, would you say?"

"I would say you had no idea of what was naughty and what was not."

He was right. I remembered being surprised at how easily everyone accepted the categories of good and bad. Most things had seemed not important enough for such classifications. Probably Mr. Taylor thought it was a bad thing to be alone with a young woman in her room. Yet soon he would be back in the basement with his wife, and they would sit polishing tarnished silverware, silently judging those who brought life to the house.

Twelve

James returned the next afternoon. Because he had found no indication that Grandmother had gone to Lake George, he decided to notify the police of her disappearance.

Two detectives from the Missing Persons Bureau visited us after dinner. They listened to our story in the way they would have listened to a smiling, beautiful woman who was speaking a language they didn't understand. They nodded politely, not wanting their boredom to be apparent. They looked at Grandmother's broken mirror, but seemed to find the elaborate clutter of her room of more significance. She would show up in a day or two, they assured us. She was probably visiting a friend. But they would do some checking anyway.

Frances failed to appear that night, and I began to think I might never see her again. But even though I wanted her to visit me, I knew I no longer needed her. Maybe she had given me everything it was in her power to give me.

Before I went to the attic for my reunion with James, I stopped at Keith's room.

"I was wondering how your snakes are," I said.

He was flattered. "My scarlet king is shedding its skin," he said. The girlish treble of his voice was tinged with a harshness that could have been either excitement or intimations of manhood.

He brought me a garishly marked red, black, and yellow

snake. The skin around its head had split and loosened. Keith took the opaque, papery skin between his fingers and peeled it back. He looked pleased.

"Have you named your snakes?" I asked.

"Yes."

I think he was embarrassed.

"What is this one called?"

"Martha."

That was Grandmother's name.

"Do you miss Grandmother?" I asked.

"I was afraid of her. Will she come back?"

"No, Keith."

He smiled and put his smooth, thin arms around me. A box on his dresser was full of cast-off, disintegrating snake skins.

I believe we were all happy during the next few days, and no one spoke of Grandmother. And then one morning Miss Barton said to me, "I had lunch with your grandfather yesterday."

I pretended I was not interested enough to reply.

She continued: "He's worried about your grandmother. He doesn't think we are doing enough to find her."

"I thought he never wanted to see her again."

"I don't believe he does. But he wants to know where she is."

"I think he's strange."

"Not really. Apparently your grandmother did something he can never forgive her for. But they did have many good years together, and he hasn't forgotten that. He's a good man, really."

I don't know what made Miss Barton think she knew anything about men. She was afraid of them physically, and she was willing to believe they had a strength that was beyond her understanding. She could accept their most obvious deceptions even after the weeks she had spent with us.

"Perhaps Grandfather had something to do with the disappearance," I said.

"Why would you think that?"

"It's possible, isn't it? I've seen him looking out of his office window at night—standing alone in the dark."

"There's nothing wrong in that. And even if you think it eccentric, you shouldn't condemn him for that. I've told you before that you should be more tolerant, Elizabeth."

I suppose Miss Barton thought it was part of her job to give me moral instructions, but I didn't understand the distinctions she made. She never spoke to me of James's visits to my room or of Katherine's visits to hers. It was as if she thought private acts were less important than public ones. I wondered what she would say if I told her about Frances. Perhaps one day I would.

"Do you know anything about what happened to Mrs. Cuttner? Anything you aren't telling us, Elizabeth?"

"I have no idea where she is," I said.

"Don't you want us to find her?"

"Maybe she doesn't want to be found."

Miss Barton was beginning to assume her insufferable, disapproving schoolteacher look. "Perhaps someone has injured your grandmother," she said. "Don't you think that person should be punished?"

I thought it was time to end the conversation. "Yes. But I don't see that there is anything I can do to help." I touched her hand. "You let me know if you think of something I can help with," I said. "In the meantime, let's not be unhappy."

"I've never been happier," Miss Barton said, and we returned to our lessons. She began to speak of the Children's Crusade. Thousands of children were sent to deliver the Holy Land, in the belief that innocence could succeed where other forces had failed. The children died.

James was busy in those days, spending a great deal of time consulting with Grandfather and with lawyers. He spoke to me even less often than usual, which pleased me, for I had no interest in his thoughts. He had been trained, as my father had been, to concern himself only with business and his appetites. With my father, business had taken precedence, and with James, his appetites. As Katherine had learned, to someone who took no interest in James's appetites, he was unbearable.

A few nights after his visit to the lake, James announced that we should assume Grandmother would not be returning to us. There were many legal complications involved, he said, but he saw no reason why we should not continue to live as we had lived before.

Later, when he was alone with me, he asked me never to leave him. I was sure he had asked the same thing of his wife once, when her body was still firm and young. "I hope I never have to leave," I said. I meant it, but it was the house, not James, that I wanted to stay with.

Even though I knew I no longer needed Frances, I still felt uncomfortable without her, and each night I spent some time before the mirror, hoping she would appear. I began to spend more time with Miss Barton in the evenings because of her resemblance to Frances. It was my desire to see Frances that was to bring confusion and pain into my life.

Thirteen

The confusion began late one night when I went to the attic. I had awakened from an uneasy sleep and remembered that I had been dreaming of Frances. In the dream I had been in the attic, watching Frances in the dusty old mirror. She had been holding a sieve and a pair of scissors and was sitting across a table from a man who held a small leather purse. The man opened the purse and emptied some small glittering objects onto the table. Frances was speaking, but I couldn't understand her words. She closed her eyes, and her lips moved slowly and repeatedly in the same pattern, as though she were speaking a single word. Although I could not hear the word, I felt it was a person's name.

After I awakened I realized that the man who had sat across the table from Frances bore a strong resemblance to me. I wanted desperately to see Frances.

I lay in the darkness listening to the sounds that came from Miss Barton's room. I think she seldom slept, and I often heard her moving about in her room. There were occasional gasps and the rush of running water.

I thought of the mirror in the attic and of the times I had seen Frances there. I got up and put on a nightgown and went out of my room and up the stairs.

The rug had been moved from its usual position. I replaced it and sat before the mirror.

"Frances," I said. "Where have you gone?"

There was no answer, and I saw only my own image. My body was visible where it touched the cool, sheer material of my gown.

"Aren't you pleased with me? I rid us of Grandmother. I did as you instructed. We're happy here now. Why don't you join us?"

A voice came from the doorway: "Elizabeth! What have you done?"

I looked at the figure that stood there, and for a moment I thought it was Frances, but it was not. It was Miss Barton.

"What is it you did to your grandmother? And who is Frances?"

There was nothing I could say.

"Speak to me, Elizabeth."

"Go away. I don't question your private acts. You mustn't question mine."

Miss Barton came toward me, pulling the door closed behind her. "My private acts are trivial. Everything I do is trivial," she said. "But that can be a virtue, my dear. It means what I do is also harmless."

She sat next to me and gently pushed back my hair, resting her hand on the back of my neck. "Who is Frances?" she asked.

I wondered whether I should tell the truth. I had thought of Miss Barton as a threat when she first came to live with us, but now I knew her to be harmless, as she had just admitted. Perhaps her physical resemblance to Frances meant she was a sort of reverse image that complemented rather than threatened the person I saw in the mirror. In any case, I knew I held the position of power. If it became necessary, I could deal with Miss Barton in the way I had dealt with Grandmother. But there were easier ways: I could have James dismiss her, or I could simply smile and place her hand on my breast. She was a most manageable person, and perhaps it would be enjoyable to have a confidante.

"Do you love me, Miss Barton?" I asked. Her hand moved involuntarily on my neck. I had spoken her sacred word. As far as I could understand it, love was no more rational and certainly of less practical value than what I had learned from Frances. Yet those who would scoff at my abilities would do the most foolish things in the name of love.

"I'm very fond of you, Elizabeth." Her hand began to tremble slightly.

"I must have your trust if I'm to answer the questions you have asked me—your trust and understanding." Actually, of course, I needed no such thing, but I was speaking of concepts she respected, and I wanted her to take me seriously.

"You can trust me," she said. "I only want to help you, if I can."

"Very well," I said.

I removed her hand from my neck and moved to face her, sitting cross-legged and feeling like a shaman at a tribal campfire, about to reveal the highest secrets. Miss Barton crossed her legs awkwardly in front of her and looked at me intently, glancing down occasionally at the front of my nightgown, at the half-concealed roundness and dark shadows.

The house was totally silent now, and I spoke softly, telling of Frances' first appearance, of my parents, and of the disappearance of Grandmother. Miss Barton listened without interrupting. Small vertical lines appeared between her eyes, and her lips parted slightly.

When I had finished speaking we sat in silence for a time. Miss Barton finally tried to speak, but she produced only a distorted whisper. She cleared her throat and said, quietly, "My poor darling. Do you want me to believe that you are a witch?"

"Those who don't understand my powers might call me that, but I don't use that word. It's a term used out of fear and misunderstanding."

"Don't you think there could be other explanations for some of the things that have happened? The drowning of your parents could have been an accident, and you don't really know what happened to your grandmother."

"Do you think I imagined Frances?" I asked.

"I think it's possible."

"But I can prove I didn't," I said. "She has given me her mark."

I raised my nightgown. The mark was scarlet against my pale thigh. Miss Barton stared in silence for a long moment, and then she turned away. She blinked several times, and I could see tears in her eyes. I took her hand and placed it against the mark. "It's real, isn't it, Miss Barton?"

She moved her stubby, short-nailed fingers over the mark. "I wish you'd call me Anne," she said.

"I don't think of you that way," I said. I moved her hand away and lowered my gown.

"Are you angry because I doubt your story?" she asked.

"No. I didn't expect you to believe me. Not right away. But you'll believe me eventually."

"I'm not sure I want to believe you. You want me to believe you've done monstrous things."

"I've just wished certain people were out of the way. Everyone has done that—you've done it. Is it so monstrous?"

"It is if you have, or believe you have, the power to give your wishes reality."

I didn't want to argue with her. The powerless always think power is evil. I stood up and gave my hand to Miss Barton, who followed me stiffly. She looked at me in a way she never had before. There was a new element in her expression: fear.

"Will you trade promises with me?" she asked.

"Of course," I said. People who ask for unspecified promises don't expect the promises to be kept.

"If I accept the possibility that your story is true," she said, "will you accept the possibility that it may not be entirely so?"

"Yes."

"And you'll seriously consider any evidence or hypotheses I present to the contrary?"

"Yes."

I realized I must leave her free to believe something other than the truth, which threatened her conventional beliefs. But by the time the sun rose she would have lain awake questioning those beliefs, and when she looked in the mirror she would shiver and wonder.

We went down the stairs, pausing at the door to her room. I whispered to her, "You look very much like Frances."

Fourteen

Katherine was unsettled at breakfast the next morning. It was obvious that Miss Barton was thinking only of me and was giving me the glances she usually reserved for Katherine.

"Miss Barton," I said, "I wonder if I might play hooky today."

"Why would you want to do that?" she asked, looking displeased. She had obviously expected to spend most of the day discussing last night's revelations with me.

Keith looked at me resentfully, envying my freedom.

Katherine liked the suggestion. "You two do work awfully hard," she said. "Why don't you and I go uptown together, Anne? There must be some shopping you want to do. And we could have lunch and see a movie."

Miss Barton wouldn't want to risk antagonizing Katherine. She would put on one of her shabby outfits and follow Katherine through department stores, offended by their excess: the discordant aromas of perfume counters; the lifeless racks of unworn, too-bright dresses. She would buy three pairs of white cotton panties, and she would wonder why she had never before noticed how many mirrors the stores contained.

"I don't like to establish a bad precedent," she said.

"Nonsense," said James. "Everyone needs a break now and then. Why don't we all take the day off? I'll cancel my appointments and take the children somewhere."

"I have an exam," Keith said. "I can't come."

The prospect of spending an afternoon with his father obviously didn't appeal to him. I don't think James disliked his son, but he treated him more as an abstraction than as a person. James didn't treat anyone seriously who was not sexually mature.

"What had you planned to do, Elizabeth?" Miss Barton asked me.

"Nothing in particular. I just wanted to get out of the house."

She looked offended, knowing I meant I wanted to be away from her; that I wanted to avoid the things she would have told me and asked me.

James said to Miss Barton, "Why don't you and Katherine do something frivolous? Elizabeth and I will do something educational. The Museum of Natural History, maybe. You're sure you won't come with us, Keith? We could look at snake skeletons."

Keith insisted on going to school, and Katherine and Miss Barton went on their matronly excursion.

I didn't look forward to spending so much time with James, particularly if he insisted on taking me to the museum. That would force me to talk to him and think about him: two things I had seldom done and never enjoyed. First, however, we would do what we had often done and always enjoyed.

James asked me to walk slowly up the stairs for him. He stood and watched me, apparently feeling some obscure pleasure. No matter how silly his games were, I enjoyed them—probably because they *were* games. He understood the importance of ritual and the irrational. I don't know what else he understood, but apparently he got along fairly well in the everyday world. I had seen him sign checks and dial telephones with pleasure and ease. I suspect he smiled more often than he should.

We spent some time in all the bedrooms that morning. He forced open the hinged jaws of one of Keith's snakes. We looked in Miss Barton's medicine cabinet, and he showed me some pictures he had taken of Katherine on their wedding night. It could not have been one of the happier nights of her life.

We ate lunch on the terrace at the Central Park Zoo, but I refused to look at the animals. I have never understood why so many people seem to be fascinated by animals —why they gaze at them, breed them, and even worship them. Perhaps the interest is simply an expression of guilt. Most of the people who were looking at the animals were at the same time digesting pieces of animal flesh.

"Are you happy?" James asked me.

"Is that important?"

"Yes. Because I've been trying to make you happy. I want to know if I've succeeded."

"I like my life. I like it very much, James." I didn't tell him that I would have liked my life just as much without him. I would have found another house, another devoted person. I couldn't deny, though, that his devotion was exceptional. What he didn't realize was that he was devoted to his own pleasure and not to me.

"Do you love me, Elizabeth?"

"No."

My denial pleased him.

"I wish you did," he said.

"No you don't. Lovers are unstable and dangerous."

"But I love you. Does that make me dangerous?"

"Yes."

He thought about that. I was beginning to feel uncomfortable. The sunshine was harsh, children were making unpleasant noises, and the animals stank.

James insisted that we go to the Museum of Natural History. The prospect didn't please me, for it didn't seem to me that the natural world has a history; it has an intricate past, but it is meaningless without people.

We walked quickly past rocks and bones and dusty stuffed animals, but we paused occasionally before artifacts. James, probably without knowing it, lingered at a display of primitive weapons. I stood for a few minutes before some African ceremonial objects and particularly admired an elaborately carved ivory rattle. It had a small polished-bronze mirror set into its handle, which was in the form of entwined snakes. I wondered who had held it and for what purposes.

"You're a little big to be admiring rattles," James said.

"That rattle has killed people," I said. "I'm sure of it."

"Nonsense. You don't kill people by making sinister noises. You kill them by crushing their skulls."

"The simple and obvious isn't the only way."

"It's usually the most efficient."

"Do you think that's what happened to Grandmother?" I asked.

James looked displeased for the first time that day. "We don't know what happened to her, do we?" he said.

I wondered what James felt about the disappearance. It had caused him no particular inconvenience and had given him control of the household. Yet it was possible that he had been fond of her.

"Did you love your mother?"

"No. She would never allow that. But sometimes when we were alone she would touch me. She wouldn't let me touch her. She would run her fingertips over my face and talk about the past. I knew I wasn't to love her, but there was a special silent bond between us."

I reached up and put my fingertips on his cheek.

When we got back to the house, Katherine and Miss Barton were in the study. Miss Barton's feet were bare, and she was flushed. Katherine asked Mr. Taylor to bring us some tea. The four of us sat quietly, occasionally smiling. Katherine poured pale smoke-flavored tea into translucent cups, and we waited for sunset.

In a few minutes Mr. Taylor reappeared. He glanced at me and then said to James, "Mr. Cuttner would like to see you. He's waiting in the foyer."

James looked alarmed. "My father?"

"Why don't we ask him in for tea?" asked Katherine.

"I'm not sure it's a social visit," said James. "He hasn't been in this house since I was a child. I'd better see what he wants."

James and Mr. Taylor left the room. I didn't know how James felt about having his father in the house. They had worked together for some years, and James had told me he was eventually to be given control of the Cuttner business. But I imagined they seldom mentioned their family relationship.

As we waited for James to return, Miss Barton avoided looking at me, and her cup rattled almost imperceptibly in her saucer.

Mr. Cuttner and James came into the room, smiling falsely.

"Father wanted to know if we had any news about Mother," James said. "I thought we might as well talk about it over tea."

Mr. Cuttner greeted us, but he was distracted by the room. The heavy old furniture, the books, and the objects assembled by generations of his family were probably more real and moving to him than the comparatively unfamiliar people were.

"It hasn't changed. Not at all," he said.

"The room, you mean?" said James. "No. I don't think it ever occurred to any of us to change it."

"I thought I might never see it again," Mr. Cuttner said.

He seemed to be drawing strength from the room. For the moment he seemed to have forgotten his body's failing organs and the milk stain on his necktie.

"I'm afraid there's no word about Mother," James said.

Mr. Cuttner wasn't listening. No one was listening. I think we were all wondering whether my grandfather was reasserting his claim on the house. That would not have been wise of him.

He stood up and began to walk slowly around the room. "People change too quickly," he said. "There is no permanence in them." He went to the wall and stood before a mirror that was mounted in the hardware of a ship's porthole. "She would look at herself in this before going in to dinner. Touching her hair."

I realized that Grandfather was a greedy man. I wondered whether most greed, like his, grew out of the belief that there was a sort of immortality in the ownership of things—things that had more stability than a human life could have. He should have known better than that. He was a Christian, and he must have been taught that the spirit is supreme. He picked up a piece of uncarved, polished jade that decorated a table. He was savoring its permanence. I, too, had held that jade. I had seen two young men, one of them holding a metal-studded leather belt.

Before Grandfather left us, he put the jade in the pocket of his coat.

That night, after James left my room, Miss Barton knocked on my door. She wore the dress she had worn earlier that day. The material at her armpits, which had been pale and stiff at breakfast, was now dark and damp.

"I want to tell you something before you go to sleep," she said. I thought she would be angry with me for having avoided her all day, but she smiled warmly. I invited her in, and she went to the bed and sat down. "I want to talk about Frances," she said.

"You'll never convince me she doesn't exist."

"No. I won't try. I only want to convince you that I know something about her. I wasn't honest with you last night, but now I think I must be if I am to help you. Come with me."

Miss Barton put her arm around me and led me to the mirror. "Tell me what you see," she said.

I was too strong to be terrified by what I saw, but I felt my muscles grow rigid. In the mirror I could see only one image: my own. The body that I felt pressing against my side and that I could see peripherally did not appear in the mirror.

I pushed free of Miss Barton's grasp and backed against the wall. She looked at me calmly and regretfully.

"Tell me whom I resemble," she said.

I couldn't answer.

"You hadn't realized, had you? We are of the same strain, Elizabeth. We are the daughters of Frances. But you must learn to deny that heritage, as your grandmother and I did."

"No. I don't believe you."

"You'll learn to believe," she said, and she slowly began to unzip her dress. She pulled it down from the top, slipping her arms out of the sleeves. She reached back, unhooked her bra, and removed it. In the hollow just above her pendulous, hard-nippled breasts was a red mark identical to the one on my leg.

"It can't be true," I said. "I would have known."

"You were too absorbed in your own condition, my dear; too concerned with your own limited knowledge."

I could not accept this woman as anything but ordinary and weak. She was clever, perhaps, but in the most commonplace way. She stood before me, ludicrously half-clothed, wanting me to deny what meant most to me. She finally realized that I did not share her excited pleasure, and she put her arms back into her dress.

"We'll speak more in the morning," she said. "Think about what you have seen, my dear. And remember this: you are powerless against me, as you were against your grandmother."

She left the room, her shabby bra dangling foolishly from her hand.

I picked up a lipstick and began to draw a large, carefully proportioned circle on my mirror. Inside the circle I wrote: "Anne Barton."

Fifteen

"Good morning, Elizabeth."

Miss Barton sat at the breakfast table, smiling. I wanted to run from the house, but I smiled back at her and watched her put a vitamin capsule in her mouth and sip some orange juice. A fragment of orange pulp stuck to the corner of her mouth. Katherine reached over and brushed it away with a napkin. I had lost my appetite.

I went to the study and waited for Miss Barton to join me. I was prepared to listen to her, no matter how disturbing or preposterous her remarks might be. I was certain she would reveal a flaw and that I could use it to restore the balance we had so carefully established.

She entered the room quietly. Her foolish smile had faded. "I know you're hurt," she said. "I don't want you to be. I just want you to know how I came to be here, and I want us to discover what has become of your grandmother."

I wasn't sure whether she meant to be condescending or not, but that is how she seemed to me.

She continued: "The women of our family have had to contend with the legacy of Frances' power since her death in the sixteenth century. That power can bring only pain and destruction to those who do not resist it. Those who have accepted it have suffered. It can easily be denied, as it has been by me and your grandmother. She knew you were vulnerable, and she brought me here to help you protect yourself. I hope you can accept that help."

"Why should I accept it?" I said. She wanted me to swallow sweaty vitamin capsules each morning and pretend James was a faithful, admirable husband. She wanted me to become an old woman who was afraid of the present. "Why should I trade strength for weakness?"

"The strength is not yours," she said. "The power belongs to Frances. She would use you and perhaps destroy you."

"Can you tell me why Frances no longer visits me?"

"It may be that you have unconsciously rejected her. She will appear only when you are receptive to everything she represents. Do you really feel no shame or regret at the thought that you might have been involved in the deaths of people who were close to you and loved you?"

"I have never wished anyone dead. I have only exposed them to Frances' power."

"Frances could not have harmed your grandmother."

"Then what happened to her?"

"That's what we must find out. We must question everyone about what they saw that night."

Miss Barton wanted to play detective. She was afraid of the truth and was searching for a conventional explanation, no matter how inadequate. Perhaps the reason she and so many others had a passion for the commonplace was that they had once seen the truth and had been terrified by it.

I had stood in the darkness of Castle Clinton and

wrapped my hand around a chill reptilian body. That was truth.

Miss Barton touched my hand. I was aware that she had been speaking, but I had not understood her. She repeated her words: "There is another way. Have you been shown scenes of violence?"

"There are objects that show me things."

"Have you touched anything in your grandmother's room?"

"No."

"Come with me."

We went upstairs. The door to Grandmother's room was ajar, the window shutters had been opened, and bright morning light illuminated the clutter of objects accumulated by the old woman over long, private years. Mr. Taylor stood in the center of the room. He was holding a long black net stocking, and his mouth was open in surprise.

"I've been straightening things up a bit," he said.

The fragments of the broken mirror were gone.

I said to Mr. Taylor, "I wonder if you could come back later."

"Yes," he said. "If you'd like." He looked around for a place to put the stocking. I took it from him, and embarrassed and irritated, he left the room.

Miss Barton sat on the bed, and I closed the shutters and turned on the gaslight. I looked slowly about the room. On every surface and along every wall were stacked objects that revealed Grandmother's life in the way the layers of shards and trash in an archeological site revealed the lives of former inhabitants.

Books, letters, and newspaper clippings were laid in random piles, partially concealing other objects: a torn gray-stained scarf; a medicine bottle half-filled with misshapen brown capsules; a riding crop, its leather handle discolored by sweating hands; a pipe stem bearing yellowish indentations where gold-filled teeth had clamped it; a pearl-handled pocketknife, its blade corroded; the intricate skeleton of a tiny animal.

I went to the frame that had held the mirror. A few pieces of slivered glass remained along its inner edges. I removed one of the pieces and placed it on the palm of my right hand. After a moment my hand began to tremble, and the room seemed to darken. I saw Grandmother's face. Her eyes were wide with fright, and she raised her hand as if to keep someone or something away from her. Another hand, larger and stronger than hers, suddenly grasped her wrist and pulled her hand away. Her face vanished, and I saw the flash of a quickly descending silver candlestick. I heard a thumping, cracking sound and a strangulated gasp. Then there was darkness.

"Elizabeth?" Miss Barton was standing at my side. "Are you all right?"

I gradually became aware of a sharp pain in my right hand, which was clenched at my side. I raised it and saw blood oozing from between the fingers. Miss Barton straightened out my fingers and removed the glass, which had embedded itself in my palm. She led me to the adjoining bathroom, where she washed and bandaged the small wound.

"What did you see?" she asked.

"It was confused. Grandmother was being attacked by someone. He hit her with a silver candlestick."

"Who hit her?"

"I couldn't see him."

"You're sure it was a man?"

"I only saw a hand, but it seemed to belong to a man."

"But you don't know who the man was?"

"No."

We went back into the bedroom and sat together on the edge of the bed.

"Are you frightened?" Miss Barton asked. She was breathing heavily.

"No," I said. I was not frightened, but I was confused. What I had witnessed was overpoweringly real, and it was undeniably a scene of death.

"You must look again," Miss Barton said.

She held the piece of glass out to me hesitantly. I took it between two fingers, avoiding its sharp edges, and instantly I saw the violent act again in exactly the way I had seen it the first time. Even without the element of surprise, the vision was shocking.

Miss Barton was staring at me anxiously, and I had dropped the fragment of glass.

"Did you see the same thing?" she asked.

"Yes."

"You didn't recognize the man?"

"No."

We sat in silence for a moment. I wanted to be alone to consider the meaning of what I had seen. Could it be true that I had not caused Grandmother's disappearance? I felt Miss Barton's thigh touching mine, and I turned to look at her. In the dim light her resemblance to Frances was strong, and I wished she were Frances so that I could question her.

Miss Barton was not conscious of me. She was looking carefully about the room. "I don't see a silver candlestick," she said.

"No. But most of the other rooms have at least one," I recalled.

"Yes. And I'm sure I remember seeing one here—on the dresser. It's been removed."

"Perhaps." Her detection didn't interest me. "I think I'll go to my room and rest," I said.

We went upstairs. As Miss Barton went into her room I could see on a table next to her bed a heavy silver candlestick.

Sixteen

I lay on my bed and listened to the sounds from the street. In spite of the continual noise of passing trucks and automobiles, it was still possible to hear the voices and even the footsteps of people who moved along the narrow street —people who spoke of business or of what they had read in the morning newspaper. I have seldom heard anyone say anything really important in the daylight or when more than one other person was present. I wished I could hear the thoughts of those who walked alone—those who were not thinking of business, but of those things they would never mention to anyone.

Occasionally I would recall what I had seen in Grandmother's room. I tried to identify the hand I had seen grasping her wrist. Could it have been James's hand: strong, gold-ringed and hairless? Mr. Taylor's: stubby and warted? Mr. Cuttner's: blue-veined and stiff? Mr. Hurlbut's: weathered and dirty-nailed? I couldn't tell. The hand had been masculine but anonymous. I remembered that Miss Barton's hands were masculine.

I resented my thoughts, and I resented Miss Barton, who had made them necessary. If balance and contentment were to be restored to the household, she would have to be mollified. I supposed she thought of herself as being particularly virtuous because she had rejected power. I imagined her at that moment standing unkempt and proud before the bathroom mirror that reflected only the door behind her. I think people who suppose themselves virtuous eventually become ridiculous because of the unending self-deception they must practice.

I longed for the simple directness of Frances.

I got up and went downstairs, where I met Katherine. She and I seldom spoke, but I knew she was disturbed by the tensions that were developing in the house, and I wanted to reassure her. I usually found her simplicity disturbing because it was founded on a lack of perception, but occasionally, as then, her naïve good will was attractive.

"I was going for a walk," I said. "Would you like to come with me, Mother?"

It embarrassed her when I called her that, because she knew the thought was ludicrous in all but the legal sense.

"Why yes, dear. I'll be with you in a moment." She went to her room and came back carrying an expensive-looking purse that was probably made from the skin of an extremely rare and timid animal. She was putting on a pair of pale-blue cloth gloves. I wondered if she had worn gloves on the day when James first had the incredible thought that it might please him to have her in his house and in his bed.

We went outside, and Katherine's manner changed immediately. She always seemed more relaxed among the unnoticing passers-by on the street than she did in the house, with its demands and confrontations.

"Where would you like to go?" Katherine asked.

"Oh, it doesn't matter."

"I have some grocery shopping to do, if you don't mind."

We walked west toward a little shop that supplied us with coffee, tea, and peculiar imported foods. I have never been interested in food, but Katherine found it exciting. What she thought of as her devotion to subtle, distinctive flavors was possibly another, more complex kind of interest. I had seen her in the kitchen with Mrs. Taylor, touching slimy and elastic flesh. Squid and tripe interested her particularly.

"Are you happy with us?" Katherine asked me.

"I couldn't imagine living anywhere else," I said. The palm of my hand throbbed slightly under its bandage.

"I think we are all happy to have you with us. Until this trouble with Mother, it seemed to me we had become a most enviable family. I do hope Mother is all right."

"You have no idea what's become of her?" I asked.

"No. Not the slightest. I never understood her very well, of course, but I can't imagine her leaving us. Or wanting to send you away to school."

"I wouldn't have liked to leave," I said. "Miss Barton and I get along so well. In a way, she's like a sister to me."

Katherine colored slightly and glanced at me. "I'm glad you feel that way," she said. She didn't want to talk about Miss Barton or about Grandmother. In fact, it was part of her peculiar charm that she seldom talked about any person. She seemed to think of people in the way most of us think about elimination—as something one is unavoidably involved with but which is not to be talked about.

The store had the penetratingly sour smell of coffee beans—an aroma that seemed more animal than vegetable and reminded me of the cages of small mammals in the zoo.

As Katherine gave the clerk her order, a small black-and-white cat that had been lying half-awake in a corner raised its head and stared at me. It came quickly over and began to rub against my legs, purring loudly.

"Do you like cats?" Katherine asked.

"I don't know," I said. "I've never lived with one."

"Miss Barton likes them, I think. She was here with me last week, and that same cat rubbed against her the way it's doing with you now. She seemed quite taken with it."

As Katherine finished giving her order, I stooped down and stroked the cat's narrow, bony skull. I felt more peaceful than I had in days.

"It looks as if you two don't want to part," Katherine

said. She reached down with one of her gloved hands to touch the cat, and it retreated quickly to its corner. She looked annoyed for a moment and then asked me, "Would you like to own a cat?"

The idea didn't appeal to me particularly, but I could see that Katherine was enjoying the thought of a new kind of shopping. "Maybe," I said.

"Why don't we get one right now? There's a fascinating pet store just a few blocks from here. I haven't been there for years."

The store turned out to be enormous, noisy, and filthy. Sullen, unhealthy animals and birds stared out at us from cramped cages. A molting macaw swayed from side to side on its perch, screaming continually. A young chimpanzee, its eyes glazed in anger, pounded the bars of its cage with a metal cup.

Katherine was frightened. Perhaps she was imagining, as I was, what the store was like at night, when the red neon sign buzzed in the window and some creatures burrowed in the soiled strips of newspaper in the bottoms of their cages while others stared hungrily into the darkness.

A young person, not clearly either male or female, asked if we were being helped. I decided to think of the person as a man, and wondered whether Katherine had made the same decision. I doubted it. The clerk was a slender, light-skinned Negro with long, almost black hair. He showed us a number of cats, most of them young, nervous, and ridiculously expensive. Katherine was attracted to a group of three Abyssinians, and though they were calmer and more elegant than most of the other breeds, they seemed insipid and self-absorbed to me.

I had almost decided to let Katherine make the choice, when I saw in a cage that had seemed empty an enormous reddish, long-haired cat lying in the shadows. It was slowly moving its tail, and it stared directly at me with narrowed pale-green eyes. I felt as though someone had touched the base of my spine with a piece of cold metal.

"I think the young lady has made her choice," the clerk said.

"Yes," I said.

The young man opened the cage door, and I reached inside with my bandaged hand. The cat placed its paw on the bandage and slowly extended its claws, pulling the bandage free and revealing the wound on my palm.

"Yes," I repeated. "I like this one."

I replaced the bandage and ran my hand through the cat's thick fur. It turned on its back, and I stroked its belly. It was a male.

As we were leaving the store the clerk handed me a business card and said, "Please let me know if I can help you in any other way." The card was imprinted with a name, address, and telephone number. The name was John Dickson.

We took the cat home in a carrying case that had a transparent plastic top. I carried it, and as we walked I glanced into the case occasionally. The cat had curled up peacefully, and I thought I could feel the faint vibrations of its purring through the handle of the case.

"What will you call it?" asked Katherine.

"I'm not sure—Scratch perhaps."

"That doesn't seem very appropriate. He seems so gentle."

"He does have claws, though. I'll call him Mr. Scratch."

"That's even worse. Isn't that a name for the Devil?"

"Oh, is it?"

When we arrived home and opened the carrying case, Scratch went immediately up the stairs and sat at the door to my bedroom. I followed and let it into the room. It jumped to the top of the dresser and sat before the mirror. A beam of sunlight fell on its back, intensifying the orange shades of its fur to a flamelike brilliance. It began to move its head from side to side and made a low-pitched sound that resembled a woman's moan.

"Hush, my dear," I said.

When the sound continued, I took the cat in my arms, sat on the bed, and lowered the trembling body to my lap. The moaning gradually subsided. Beneath the thick fur was a lean, strong body that transmitted a pleasing warmth through the thin material of my skirt.

"There," I said. "We'll please each other."

The moan had become a purr.

James didn't like the cat and refused to have it in the room when we were together. The others in the house seldom saw it, since it was content to stay in my room, curled on my bed, relaxed but alert, looking out through barely opened eyes as if waiting to be summoned for an important task. Miss Barton disapproved of my keeping any kind of animal, but Scratch was fond of her, and she was unable to keep from touching him.

Seventeen

The household settled into a comfortable routine, and I think we all would have been happy to the extent that we were able had it not been for Miss Barton's concern with Grandmother's disappearance. She spoke of it every day, at dinner and during my lessons. She had found out from Mr. Taylor that there had been a silver candlestick in Grandmother's room and that it had disappeared.

I was apparently the only one who had been absent from the house at any time on the night of the disappearance and, as I knew, Mr. Cuttner had been in his offices next door.

Miss Barton had been having lunch regularly with Mr. Cuttner. I think in his obtuseness he imagined she was attracted to him. I joined them for lunch one day. We went to a seafood restaurant near the Fulton Fish Market. We walked through the market area first. At midday it was practically deserted, with only its stench and discarded fish heads and guts left to indicate the activity of the early-morning hours. Half-wild cats and large, aggressive gulls scavenged among the slimy leavings. As we walked Mr. Cuttner's hand occasionally brushed against Miss Barton's girdled hip.

In the restaurant Mr. Cuttner ordered a lobster, and engrossed himself in cracking, probing, and sucking. Miss Barton now and then asked him questions about his life with Grandmother. He ignored most of them. I decided she was being too cautious, and I asked the question she was afraid to ask: "Grandfather, why did you leave Grandmother?"

He paused, holding a lobster claw in midair. "I don't talk about that," he said.

"I know. But everyone wonders about it. The truth can't be as bad as the speculations."

I thought he was going to tell me to be quiet and eat my lunch. But he looked at me closely. His jaw was slack and he breathed noisily. He seemed to realize that despite the difference in our ages, I was not a child, but a woman—a woman he wanted to please.

"Everyone assumes there was another man," I said.

Grandfather's face reddened. I think he wanted to throw the lobster claw at me, but he said, "And who does everyone assume the other man was?"

"They don't know," I said. "But I know."

Miss Barton had been looking at me with a combination of disapproval and fascination. "How could you know such a thing?" she asked.

"I saw him," I said. "He visited her."

"You know who the visitor was?"

"Of course."

"But why didn't you tell us?"

"Because it wasn't anyone's business. It wasn't my business either. I won't say who it was unless Grandfather wants me to."

Grandfather looked at me with new respect—or possibly with fear. Then he began to laugh. He dropped his lobster claw and continued to laugh. People around us interrupted their conversations to look at him. I remembered Mr. Hurlbut's solemn, strong face as he left Grandmother's room. He obviously had never laughed hysterically in his lifetime. I knew, as Grandmother had known, that he was incomparably superior to Mr. Cuttner.

"It will be our secret," I said when Grandfather had stopped laughing. I no longer had to worry about his meddling. He would be my generous friend.

After lunch Miss Barton and I spent the afternoon in the study. She was disturbed that I had information she felt she needed for her "investigation," and she asked me repeatedly to tell her the name of Grandmother's visitor. It was an unpleasant afternoon. Miss Barton's nostrils were flared and her eyes were narrowed. A little bulge of fat encircled each of her thighs where her girdle ended.

I wanted us to speak gently about Frances and her descendants. I wanted to remind Miss Barton of the pleasures she had rejected. I wanted to restore her courage, to have her accept her heritage. I began to realize, however, that we would not share such afternoons until I resolved her anxiety over Grandmother's disappearance. And I wondered whether I might be unable to see Frances again until the matter was settled.

"Anne," I said.

Miss Barton stopped talking, looked puzzled for a moment, and then smiled. I had used her given name.

"Anne, aren't there people—our kind of people—who can reveal the truth? And wouldn't it be better to get the help of such a person than to spend any more afternoons like this?"

"I suppose there are still such people. They were called cunning folk in the sixteenth century. But I'm trying to convince you that such methods are not necessary."

"What did cunning folk do?"

"They had the power to find lost objects and to cure illness."

"Were they considered witches?"

"Not generally, I think. Their powers were supernatural but didn't necessarily derive from the Devil. They were more likely to be accused of white witchcraft than of practicing the black art." Miss Barton was obviously as interested in the subject as I was and probably for the same reason, although I supposed she was pretending her interest was only historical.

"Did they have a ritual?"

"They used magic words and formulas, and some objects: mirrors, or a sieve and scissors."

"Do you know anyone who can do those things?" I suspected she did, but I didn't expect her to admit it.

"No," she said. "I knew of people in England, but not here."

I would have to find someone on my own.

We were silent for a moment, and then she said, "Thank you."

"For what?"

"For calling me Anne."

She was easily pleased.

The next day I received a telephone call. It was from the clerk in the pet store.

"This is John Dickson," he said, in a voice that was as sexually ambiguous as its owner's appearance. "I was wondering whether there were any problems with the cat you purchased from us. We like to be sure our customers are fully satisfied."

"That's thoughtful of you," I said. "I have no complaints at all. You sold me a remarkable animal."

"Yes. That's what I thought. Well, I won't disturb you any further. But if you have any questions—if there's any information you need—give me a call at any time."

"Yes. Thank you."

I hung up, wondering why the truth about the world was so seldom told; why we heard so much about congressmen and bank presidents and others who wielded commonplace power and so little about those who had other powers.

As I stood at the telephone, James came up behind me and put his hands on my shoulders. "Come upstairs," he said. He could have been a congressman.

Eighteen

I went to the pet shop the next day. John Dickson was busy with a customer when I arrived, and I watched him carefully as he moved through the shop. He was wearing a loose shirt and tight blue jeans. He had the pelvis and hips of a man but he moved them as a woman would. The total effect was somehow not feminine, however, and I found him strangely attractive. When he was free, he smiled and came toward me.

"Hello, Elizabeth," he said. "I was hoping you'd stop in. I have a message for you from Martha."

"I thought you might. Can you give me the message now?"

"No. Actually, the message is incomplete. If you visited me at my apartment tonight, I think I could complete it for you."

"I can do that," I said.

"It would help if you brought some small belonging of Martha's."

"At what time?"

"Would eight be all right?"

"Yes. At the address on your card?"

"Yes. Until tonight."

As I turned to go I lowered my eyes and glanced once more at the lower part of his body. The effect had changed. It was a prominent and masculine change.

It rained that night, and the streets of the Upper West Side of Manhattan were almost as deserted as those in my neighborhood. I had taken the subway uptown, and the trip had left me disturbed and excited as it always did. I had never understood how so many people seemed to ride the subway trains in apparent lethargy. The sound of metal wheels screeching on tracks, the enclosed darkness of the tunnels, and the mysterious, impersonal opening and closing of the train doors made me feel I was in some sort of hostile underworld. People entered the train, bringing with them the odor of damp clothing. They sat staring at their reflections in the windows opposite them, propping up dripping umbrellas that left little dark puddles on the floor.

I left the train at Eighty-sixth Street and emerged into a world that was scarcely less oppressive than the one I had been in. Most of the stores along Broadway were dark and locked away behind folding steel gates. Men peered out into the night from the lobbies of old hotels, and bored clerks stood behind delicatessen counters where unsold potato salad lay souring in stainless steel trays. I thought of the thousands of people in the apartment buildings that surrounded me; I thought of them drinking or smoking, people trying to forget what they had done earlier and what they would do later.

John Dickson lived on the fourth floor of a neglected brownstone building on Eighty-fourth Street. There was no buzzer system and the entrance door stood open. I walked up the four flights of stairs, past flimsy doors that barely masked the sounds and odors that filled the small apartments.

I knocked on John's door, and heard a metallic scraping as he pushed aside the cover of a peephole in the door. For a moment his eye was visible, and then he clicked two locks and the door opened.

The apartment was lighted by three candles set out on small tables. The only other furniture in the room was a chest, a mattress on the floor, and three straight-backed wooden chairs. The walls were bare. John was wearing a long-sleeved gray robe, and he looked more feminine than he had previously. I realized that his sexual ambiguity resulted not from a desire to alter his sex but from an attempt to ignore it.

We sat facing each other across one of the tables. He seemed to take it for granted that there was no need to discuss why I had come or why he had invited me.

"I envy you," he said.

"Why is that?"

"My power is passive. Yours is active."

"Yet I have come to you because I need assistance."

"I'd like to be your assistant. I hope we'll meet often."

He opened a drawer in the table and brought out a pair of scissors and a handleless sieve. He placed them in front of me. I suddenly remembered that I had dreamed of this meeting. In the dream, Frances had sat in John's place.

"Have you brought me something of Martha's?" John asked.

I had removed a few more fragments of the broken mirror from its frame and put them in a small leather purse. I put the purse on the table. John reached out and inverted the sieve over the purse and then opened the scissors and placed them in front of the sieve.

"What is it you wish to know?" he asked.

"I want to know what has become of Martha and who is responsible for her disappearance."

"Give me your hands," John said.

I reached across the table and placed my hands in his. I felt an excitement growing in me that was unlike any I had experienced before, but which was similar to sexual arousal.

John's eyes were closed, and he began to make little pleasureful moaning sounds, which gradually changed to a chantlike repetition of the phrase: "Martha, come." His hands tightened on mine, and he began to gasp and choke. Then he released his grip and threw his arms up before his face. He stood up suddenly, knocking over his chair, and then moved a few steps across the room and collapsed. I went and knelt at his side. He was breathing heavily, and one of his legs was twisted beneath him. I raised his robe and straightened out the leg. It was hairless and delicately shaped.

Soon his eyes opened, and I helped him back to the table. He sat for a few seconds and then said, "Martha is dead."

"How did she die?"

"You have seen that yourself."

"Whose hand did I see?"

"It was the hand of Frances."

"No," I said. "It was a man's hand."

"Let me show you," John said. He reopened the drawer in the table and brought out a silver-handled mirror and held it before his chest so that its glass faced me. For a few seconds I saw only a gray cloudiness, and then the image of a face began to form.

"This is Frances," John said.

I saw James's face in the mirror.

I began to laugh.

John was looking at me impassively, but I realized my laughter must have offended him.

"I'm sorry," I said. "There is some confusion."

"There is no confusion. There is no error."

"I'm the one who is confused," I said. "What you have shown me is clear enough. I'm grateful."

"I'm glad I could help," John said. He looked at me in a way I was not used to. It was a look of respect and affection, but there was no possessiveness or selfishness in it. It made me feel uncomfortable.

I listened to the sounds from other apartments: loud laughter; repetitive, graceless music; thin, distorted voices from the soundtrack of an old movie. The candlelight flickered over the bare surfaces of the room. It was like being in a chapel. I didn't like chapels.

I took a fifty-dollar bill from my pocket and placed it on the table in front of John. He smiled and pushed it back toward me.

I began to feel angry. I picked up the bill and held it over the flame of the candle that stood on the table. As the money burned, John began to laugh. It was harsh laughter, a sound more suited to a rooming house than to a chapel. John was not that much different from his neighbors.

When he realized I was not laughing with him, he stopped abruptly. He looked at me at first uncertainly and then apologetically.

"Asceticism doesn't become you, John," I said. "In my house there is a great deal of furniture. There are springs in our beds. Perhaps you would like to visit me sometime."

I left him. I knew he would not sleep well that night.

Early the next morning James came unsteadily into my room, carrying a nearly empty cognac bottle and seeking comfort and strength.

As we lay on our backs, head to foot, stroking each other, I said, "James, did you kill Grandmother?"

His hand stopped moving, but only for an instant. He answered, "Did *you*, Elizabeth?"

Nineteen

Miss Barton believed that John Dickson had revealed the truth: that James had killed Grandmother.

"John revealed nothing," I said, "except that he is subject to forces he can't control."

"But he identified James."

"He also accused Frances. Do you want me to believe that Frances acted through James?"

"No. James acted out of his own selfishness. He didn't want you to be sent away."

I was about to argue with her, when it occurred to me that I had achieved what I sought: Miss Barton had found an explanation that satisfied her. All I needed to do was to agree with her, and perhaps she would forget the matter.

"I suppose that could be true, Anne," I said. "But if so, what should we do? Do we have to accuse him or reveal him?"

She hesitated. I supposed her own selfishness was asserting itself. She wouldn't want the household to be disturbed any more than James would. "Yes," she said. "James must be punished."

Then, for the first time, it occurred to me that perhaps Miss Barton wanted James to leave us. Maybe I had underestimated her. She already controlled Katherine, and with James gone, she might imagine she could control me. I wondered if she had arranged last night's meeting with John Dickson to try to convince me of James's guilt. It could be that she herself had killed Grandmother. I looked at her masculine hands.

"Why must he be punished?" I asked. "Why couldn't we accept what he has done as an accomplished fact and go on with our lives?"

"It's a matter of simple morality. What he did was wrong."

"I think morality is only simple when you're judging someone else's actions. If you had committed a murder, would you be so eager to have the fact revealed?"

"You miss the point, Elizabeth. What any individual feels about an evil act doesn't matter. What's important is that the evil not be allowed to flourish."

I didn't want to go on with the conversation. I knew that next she would tell me how she had overcome the evil in her life. But perhaps she had exchanged one kind of evil for another that was more common.

"In any case," I said, "there is no evidence that James committed a crime."

"Evidence must exist. We simply haven't found it. You could find it, Elizabeth."

"How?"

"Question him. Search his room. He wouldn't be suspicious of you."

I thought maybe it was time I had a new tutor. What had made me so tolerant of this charmless woman and her banal talk of virtue? Why had I let her deceive me?

I locked myself in my room that afternoon, ignoring Miss Barton when she knocked on the door and called to me. Mr. Scratch sat in my lap as I practiced my flute. I played the melody I had learned from Frances, and I thought of her. Why was it I no longer saw her? Miss Barton said it was because I had stopped needing her. But that was not true now, for I felt that Frances was the only one who could resolve the confusion that surrounded me.

Had Miss Barton somehow silenced Frances? Or was James involved, as John Dickson implied? Perhaps I would find the answer only when I knew what had happened in Grandmother's room that night. Grandmother bore the mark of Frances, and both of them had vanished on the same night.

I decided I would spend the night in Grandmother's room.

After dinner the family gathered in the study. As usual, the others reflected my mood, and there was little conversation. Keith sat next to me on the sofa and whispered silly and occasionally obscene riddles into my ear. He liked to be near me, and before long he would find himself thinking more often of me than of his snakes.

His father watched us jealously and began to flirt with Miss Barton, which embarrassed us all.

When Katherine told Keith it was time for him to go to bed, I said I was going to read in my room, and I went upstairs with him. We paused outside the door to his room, and I opened my mouth slightly and placed it gently against his thin, dry lips. He pulled away from me and rushed into the bedroom. I stood outside the door and soon heard faint, unpleasant squeaks. I knew he was holding one of his doomed mice by its tail, watching as a hungry snake uncoiled.

I went to Grandmother's room.

After lighting the gas jet and locking myself in, I walked slowly around the cluttered room. I wondered why Grandmother had lived amid such voluptuous disarray when her manner and appearance had been so austere and restrained. Only one area of the room was neatly arranged: the corner that contained a large roll-top desk. Next to the desk was a glass-doored bookcase containing a series of matched ledgerlike books, each of which had a number on its spine. The numbers were arranged consecutively from one to forty.

I opened the case and took out the first volume. Inscribed in a precise handwriting on the first page were the words "The Female Descendants of Frances Williams: Volume I, 1573-1583." I looked at several other volumes and found that each covered a ten-year period and consisted of genealogical listings marked with a complex set of symbols and supplemented by occasional passages describing events in the lives of some of the women named in the listings.

Strangely, each volume seemed to contain about the same number of listings. After more browsing in the ledgers I concluded that assuming the records were reasonably complete, Frances' descendants were far from prolific. A combination of childlessness and early deaths over the four centuries had kept the number of living descendants about the same at any given time.

I deciphered all but a few of the symbols that were entered in the listings, but the most significant sign was immediately recognizable. It was the same as the mark on my thigh, and it was entered only before certain of the names. In some cases the mark had been entered and then crossed out. I looked at some of the recent volumes and found that the names Martha Cuttner and Anne Barton were both preceded by crossed-through marks. The mark before my own name was fresh and unobscured.

The descriptive passages varied from single cryptic sentences to long, detailed narratives. Death and misunderstanding were mentioned often. I looked forward to reading the ledgers. They were meant for me. They would be my tutor.

I took off my clothes and went to Grandmother's large mahogany-posted bed. I pulled back the covers and stretched my body out on the hard mattress. It was prob-

ably here that my father and James had been conceived.
I closed my eyes and listened to the occasional sounds in
the house. Someone walked past the door. Katherine gig-
gled. Then I heard a sound that seemed to be in the room
with me. It began as a faint, intermittent rustling, but as it
grew louder I recognized it as whispering. It was a woman
breathing hard and saying, "George . . . George." I opened
my eyes and looked around the room, but I was still alone.
The voice was very close.

I shut my eyes again and had a vision of two figures.
They were naked and in silhouette. I remembered what I
had seen when I had picked up the letter opener in Grandfather's office. I was seeing the same two figures again,
and as before, one of them was Grandmother as a young
woman. The figures embraced and once more I heard the
name "George" being whispered. Gradually I began to see
the couple's features. The man was George Hurlbut, the
caretaker at Lake George. They were standing in one of
the bedrooms of our cabin, and I watched intently as they
moved to the bed. The vision lasted far into the night.

I woke up before dawn and went to my own room. I
lay on the bed and stroked Mr. Scratch as I thought about
the significance of what I had seen. Mr. Hurlbut had been
Grandmother's lover and could have been the father of
James or of my own father. He visited Grandmother before
her disappearance—before she announced that I was to
return to school. He could have been responsible for her
sudden change of attitude; he could have been responsible
for her disappearance, or for her death.

I remembered that James had gone to Lake George to
look for Grandmother. Did he know about Mr. Hurlbut?
What had he expected to find at the lake? What *had* he
found there? I wondered if James and I could take a trip to
the lake together.

Twenty

I was gracious at breakfast.

"Did you sleep well, Elizabeth?" James asked me. He was wondering where I had slept. He was wearing the suit he wore when he was planning to talk to lawyers. He disliked lawyers but was afraid to offend them because he knew they controlled his life. Believing that adolescent gestures interested me, he told me once that as a mark of disrespect he never wore underwear at his legal conferences.

"Yes," I said. "I slept very well. I dreamed we were wearing bathing suits and sitting under a large umbrella—everyone at this table. Outside the shelter of the umbrella it was snowing. But we were warm, and there were flowers growing around us. Katherine was eating an orchid."

Katherine and Miss Barton smiled. Before I had invented my little image they had both looked grim. I think James must have slept with Katherine the previous night.

After breakfast I followed Mr. Taylor down to the kitchen. His wife was washing dishes, holding her white hands in the gray water among soggy fragments of uneaten bacon and disintegrating scrambled eggs. We seldom saw Mrs. Taylor, who nourished us and cleaned up after us. I suppose there is no need to speak to those whose dirt and appetites you know intimately.

"Hello, Mrs. Taylor," I said.

She looked around and nodded and then turned to look again into the greasy water. Her body was thin and unassertive, and her slack dress might have had nothing within it. I wondered what part of that body had once excited Mr. Taylor. The feet, perhaps.

"Have you ever been to Lake George, Mr. Taylor?"

"No, miss. Mrs. Taylor and I were always given time off when the family went to the lake."

"Did Grandmother go there often?"

"Quite often," he said. "She was very fond of the lake at one time." He was obviously uneasy with my questions, but he didn't try to escape from me.

"I suppose you miss my grandmother."

"No one will ever take her place," he said, and then turned away as though he had made his point.

"Of course not. But we must do as well as we can until she returns."

"And if she doesn't return, miss?"

"I think we can still be comfortable."

"I'm seldom comfortable when unexplained things happen."

"Then you must often be uncomfortable, Mr. Taylor."

"Quite often."

I thought it more likely that he was continually uncomfortable. Didn't he realize that nothing in life could be satisfactorily explained? He wanted life to be simple to the point of the ridiculous. To him, a mirror was simply a surface to be polished. He couldn't have begun to understand Grandmother's life, but he insisted on understanding her death.

"I'm sure everything will be explained eventually," I said. "That's what we all want."

"Yes, miss."

Mr. Taylor sat down at a table, picked up a cloth, and began polishing a silver candlestick.

I spent the morning looking at some of Grandmother's ledgers with Miss Barton, who had seen them many times before. When I told her I had discovered them, she looked displeased.

"I don't think there's much point in your reading that

sort of thing," she said. "It's not dramatic at all—just the statistics of a great deal of unhappiness and misfortune."

"It must be more than that. And in any case, it's our heritage, isn't it?"

"We don't have to be at the mercy of our heritage. I've rejected it, and you should, too."

"Maybe it will be easier for me if I know more about what I am expected to reject."

Miss Barton tried to look skeptical, but her expression was not convincing. When we entered Grandmother's room and pulled two chairs up to the old desk, I could see that Anne was excited—and possibly frightened.

The early records of Frances' descendants consisted primarily of notes about witchcraft trials in the County of Essex in the seventeenth century. Frances Williams had lived in the village of Hatfield Peverel. She never married, but had one daughter. This proved to be the beginning of a persistent pattern, and throughout the records there were instances of daughters being born to unwed women.

The entries created a picture of a rural society that was dominated by ignorance and fear. People were tried and imprisoned because a neighbor's livestock had become ill or because they had become "sowers of discord." Prosecutions declined in the late seventeenth century, and in 1736 there were two important events: the witchcraft statute was repealed, and the first of Frances' descendants left rural Essex and went to live in London. Thirty years later another crossed the Atlantic and settled in New York. There were three principal groups of descendants; the Essex group; the London group, to which Miss Barton belonged; and the New York group, which produced Grandmother and me.

I read through several of the ledgers carefully, but Miss Barton kept only one of them in front of her, and she constantly glanced around the room. It might have been that she was bored, having seen the books before, but she was breathing more rapidly than usual, and I suspected she was not as indifferent to her heritage as she pretended.

When it was time for lunch, she said she was not hungry and would rather take a nap. Before she left I asked her opinion of why the statutes against witchcraft had been repealed. She thought about it for a moment. It was possible she was wishing the laws were still in effect.

"I suppose," she said, "intelligent people began to believe that one person's thoughts could not harm another person."

"But that's not true, is it?"

"Yes it is, Elizabeth. The only person you can hurt with your thoughts is yourself."

"Then there's no reason to fear Frances?"

"Not for others—just for you."

"For us," I said.

James and I were the only ones in the dining room for lunch. Mr. Taylor had set out a small buffet, and James was excitedly heaping a plate with cheese when I entered the room. He was fond of cheeses, particularly of the ones that stank; not just the pungent and delicate-flavored French varieties that I liked, but overripe Liederkranz and hand cheese—what he called dirty-feet cheese. There was a bottle of wine and a plate of sliced raw onions at his place. The wine was one he was especially proud of: a raw Greek country wine he said was the only kind he knew of that would stand up to his cheese. It seemed to me it could actually have been vinegar.

James was in a buoyant mood. I took some cold ham and salad and sat next to him. He put his fingers under my nose. They reeked of the cheese he had been handling.

"The fecal finger of fate," he said, and grinned.

I frowned.

"Come with me to the opera tomorrow night," he said.

"You know opera makes me uncomfortable."

"They're doing the good one. And no one in the cast is obese."

The "good one" was *Don Giovanni*. James felt about the Don Juan legend the way a priest feels about the New Testament. I thought it might be enjoyable to go with him, after all; to glance at his awed expression, to hear his toneless grunting.

"Yes, I'll go," I said.

After lunch we went to my room. James didn't wash his hands.

When I went to read Grandmother's ledgers the next morning, I found that one of the volumes—the twentieth—was missing. There was a space where it had stood in the sequence, a space I was certain had not been there previously. Miss Barton had gone out on an errand, and I thought perhaps she had borrowed the missing volume. I continued my reading, and when I reached Volume 21, I found that it began with some pages headed: "Description of Various Efficacious Formulae and Ceremonies Employed by Frances Williams in her Arts—Continued and Concluded."

The pages that followed contained descriptions of words and phrases to be spoken and ritual acts that could be used to create specific conditions. Most of the material was petty and of little interest; how to get a cow to give sour or discolored milk; how to cause a person to grow warts or moles; how to cause a stiffness to develop in someone's arm.

The words to be spoken varied from the nonsensical to the obscene, and the rituals included "securing the subject's urine by night" and the use of assorted animal "familiars" to transmit conditions.

The descriptions were interesting but not especially useful. I suspected that the preceding material in the missing volume would contain more helpful information, and I was certain Miss Barton had removed that volume.

Twenty-one

James and I went to the opera that night. He drove us uptown in the family car—an old black Rolls-Royce that seemed to me appropriate only for funerals. We went across town toward the West Side Highway, soon reaching the piers and sheds that not too many years before had been almost constantly busy berthing transatlantic liners and cruise ships. A few of the docks were still used, and sometimes in the quiet of the night the gloomy rumbling of a liner's whistle would echo through the streets and past our house. Within the house we would pause and smile or turn in our beds.

That night, however, no ships were docked. The piers were dark, looming vaguely against the night sky. Many of the sheds were abandoned, furnishing vast, decaying shelters for derelicts and rats.

James drove intently but recklessly, getting us to the underground parking lot at Lincoln Center in minutes.

"I like the idea of entering the opera house from under the ground," he said. "It makes me feel like Orpheus."

He reminded me more of Priapus. We went through the lobby and up the staircase to the first level, where we could watch the audience arrive. James took my hand, and I felt his grip tighten involuntarily every time a particularly striking woman entered the lobby. He had almost forgotten me, and I was happy that he had. His attention was often oppressive, and it was a relief to have him concentrate on someone else's body.

I, too, watched the women entering the lobby, most of them unwisely displaying their arms, shoulders, and bosoms. I was wearing a dress I had found in Grandmother's closet. It was black, long-sleeved and full length, with tiny white buttons on the front that ran from the high neckline to the waist.

We waited until the last moment to enter the auditorium, and the ominous first notes of the overture were sounding as we took our seats. James took a pair of folding opera glasses from his pocket and watched intently as the curtain rose. I found it more satisfying to close my eyes. The people on the stage could never have done the things they had to represent. The man who played Don Giovanni had obviously spent most of the passion in his life on his voice.

James understood the role better than anyone who had ever sung it. He understood the violence and dedication of the Don, and when Leporello sang the catalog of his master's conquests, James did not smile. He was awed and envious.

During the intermissions James peered around the house with his glasses, searching out cleavages, examining shoulders. He would find what was obvious to me without the help of magnification: too many of the shoulders were dry-skinned, too many of the cleavages were shaped by desperate arrangements of wire and elastic. And if he raised his glasses slightly, he would find faces that reflected emptiness and weakness. Later he would look at me with new appreciation.

It wasn't until the final act of the opera that his interest wavered and he lowered his glasses. "Let's leave now and avoid the crowd," he whispered. His words were barely audible over the cries of Don Giovanni—cries of eternal desolation from amid engulfing flames. I didn't move.

James was silent as we drove back downtown. I closed

my eyes, trying to rid myself of the unsettling impressions
of the opera. I thought of the audience in their jewels and
overpriced clothing, and I wondered what it meant to
them to see a man overcome by supernatural forces. Some
of them were amused, I suppose, and others were indifferent. I wondered how many, like James, were frightened.

When the car stopped, I opened my eyes. We were not
at the house, but were parked beside St. Paul's Chapel,
an eighteenth-century church and graveyard occupying a
square block amid the office buildings north of our home.

I looked questioningly at James. He said, "Let's go sit in
the graveyard for a while."

"Why?" I asked. I was afraid he wanted to do something
that shouldn't be done in public.

"I have a present for you," he said. "It will be more
memorable if I give it to you there." He opened the glove
compartment and took out a brightly wrapped box.

"All right," I said, and got out of the car. James's sugges-
tions often seemed silly to me at first, but I usually ended
up enjoying them.

We walked among weather-worn grave markers whose
inscriptions were generally illegible even in daylight. I
wondered whether any of our relatives were buried there.
I could not remember Grandmother ever mentioning St.
Paul's, but it was probable that some of our ancestors had
at least attended services in the church.

We sat down on a bench along one of the dark walks,
and I remembered the churchyard scene in *Don Giovanni,*
in which the statue of a man the Don had killed threatened
revenge.

"It's too bad there are no statues here," I said.

"Why is that?"

"One of them might speak to us."

"Yes," James said. "Oh yes. It is too bad."

He turned to face me and put his hand on my throat

for a moment. Then he began to unbutton the front of my dress. I assumed he was going to expose my breasts, but he opened the dress only to a point slightly below the base of my throat. Then he handed me my present. I unwrapped the box quickly and found a strand of gray baroque pearls. There was something unpleasant about them.

"Let me put them on you," James said.

He fastened the necklace on me, and I felt the cold, oily surface of the pearls against my skin. I began to shiver. James kissed my neck, and I heard as if from a distance a ghastly whisper: "Frances. No."

And then I realized I had seen the pearls before. Grandmother had been wearing them the last time I saw her.

James either didn't notice my shivering or thought it was a symptom of pleasure. "Do you like them?" he asked.

"They're lovely," I said. "Where did you get them?"

"They've been in the family for generations."

"On Grandmother's side or Grandfather's?"

"Grandmother's. She told me they were to be worn by the most beautiful women of the family. That's why I wanted you to have them."

He knew Grandmother would not return. Otherwise he would not have given me her pearls.

What was his connection to Frances?

There was no time for me to consider such things until much later, when James lay sleeping beside me, the perspiration not yet dry on his lean, exerted body.

Mr. Scratch ran across the rug, pursuing and toying with a small, shiny object: a pearl. James had asked me not to take the necklace off, and it had broken, scattering the pearls on and around the bed.

James was snoring loudly, his mouth gaping and his jaw displaying a weakness that was never apparent when he was awake. It was as if he were in a pleasure-induced trance. I wondered whether he would have killed someone who stood between himself and such pleasure. I could not be sure, for I did not understand the kind of strength that depended on physical confrontation and the wielding of crude weapons.

Perhaps James *had* been responsible for Grandmother's disappearance. I recalled that a few nights earlier I had thought the same thing about Mr. Hurlbut. It might be if I brought the two of them together, I would learn the truth. And if I learned the truth, I might learn why Frances no longer visited me.

I grasped a few of the coarse hairs that grew thick on James's upper thigh and I tugged at them sharply. He gasped and opened his eyes.

"I want you to take me to Lake George," I whispered.

He frowned, perhaps out of annoyance at being distracted from his dreams. He once told me he dreamed frequently of making love to a "spider woman." She had six hairy arms, and her genitals were like a shark's mouth: hairless, gaping, and filled with sharp teeth. The dream gave him pleasure.

"The lake?" he said.

"Yes. Just the two of us."

"The lake isn't for us, my dear. It's for them."

"Who?"

"Our enemies," he whispered. His eyes closed again, and his breathing was deep. He was asleep in a moment.

I would persuade him in the morning, when the sunlight fell across his feet, illuminating the vein that pulsed just below his ankle bone. He would not think of enemies then.

Twenty-two

Grandfather joined us for breakfast the next morning. He spoke of his pleasure at being returned to his family. He sat next to me, occasionally touching me in an abstract way, as though I were a piece of old, expensive furniture.

He spoke of his grandson taking over the family business one day, and Keith was obviously distressed at the thought. We were all distressed. Grandfather's amiable, insensitive presence made us all aware of how much we valued the uncommon world we had established. Grandfather represented an alien world in which exceptional people were not welcome. He was not a threat to us, however, for he was meeting us on our own ground, where our strength was secure. And no matter how much he might want to make us part of his world, it was much more likely he would become part of ours.

While Grandfather was talking to Miss Barton, I excused myself and went upstairs to her room. Her bed was unmade, and a gray cotton nightgown was thrown across it. I picked up the nightgown and held it to my face. It had the same odor Miss Barton usually did: not quite clean but not unpleasant. I looked around the room, wondering where the missing ledger might be.

I went to a bookcase in the corner of the room. The books were mostly familiar to me from my studies with Miss Barton, and I felt affection for her as I looked at the generally worn bindings. There was a time when I thought there were no more mysterious and exciting objects than books. I particularly enjoyed borrowing a book from the library and examining its pages for signs that others had held it. I imagined someone lying in bed, supporting the book on his or her body, allowing a red, slightly indented line to form where its edge rested. I wondered what thoughts or feelings the words created in the previous readers. I liked to find pencil marks on pages; words and sentences underlined; check marks in margins.

I took down an anthology of English prose and leafed through it, stopping when I found an underlined passage. It was from John Selden's seventeenth-century *Table Talk:*

> The law against witches does not prove that there be any; but it punishes the malice of those people that use such means to take away men's lives. If one should profess that by turning his hat thrice, and crying "Buzz," he could take away a man's life, though in truth he could do no such thing, yet this were a just law. . . .

I replaced the book, and as I continued to look for the ledger, I thought about the struggle Miss Barton must have had in refusing the strength that was given to her. Apparently it was easiest just to deny the existence of the truth. To refuse it was to acknowledge its existence.

I went to the bulky mahogany dresser that took up most of one wall. I quickly looked into each of its drawers, running my hand under the meager layers of underclothes. They were garments that were not meant to be seen; they were neither modest nor decorative, but merely utilitarian —the clothes of a person who served her body but did not honor it.

The top drawer contained a red plastic tray that was stuffed with neglected inexpensive jewelry, most of which I had never seen her wear. I opened a tarnished locket, which contained a curl of hair. The hair was fine, a woman's hair, the color of mine.

I found the ledger on a shelf in her closet, next to a blue

straw hat. Before I left the room I put the hat on, turned it three times, and said, "Buzz."

I took the ledger to my room and sat at my writing table with it. I excitedly ran my fingers across the old half-leather binding and felt my heart begin to pound in anticipation. As I sat there, Miss Barton knocked at my door and called my name. I didn't answer, and she went away. I heard her moving about in her room, and soon she was back at my door.

"Elizabeth," she said. "Don't open the book. It can only create harm—not only for others, but for you."

I didn't answer her.

"Destroy the book, Elizabeth. Don't let it destroy you."

She was forgetting that she had had the opportunity to destroy the book and had not been able to do it. Despite what she pretended to feel, she obviously knew that the book was too important to be disposed of. It made her uncomfortable, but it was stronger than she was. She spoke my name a few more times and then went away.

As I opened the book I heard a vague, distant moan. It could have been Miss Barton lying on her disarrayed bed, feeling distress or envy. Or it could have been someone farther off in time and place, someone feeling less ordinary emotions.

The book's pages were darkened and bent at their upper-right corners. The stitching that held the pages to the boards had loosened, and fragments of dried glue dropped from the ledger's spine onto my desk. No other volume in the series had shown as many signs of use.

The text was arranged in three principal sections: a list of "words, signs, and charmes efficacious to conjuring, sorcery, and magical acts"; a description of "helpful implements and devices"; and a section specifying particular rituals and their results. The last section was subdivided into acts affecting spirit beings, animal beings, and humans. I

turned to the pages concerning spirit beings and found a
check mark beside the entry headed "To Nullify the Influence of a Spirit." The entry read:

> Go at night into the chamber of the person who is
> under the influence of a Spirit. While that person
> sleeps, employ a pair of shears to remove a lock of
> hair from the person's head. At that moment, say,
> "Spirit, I sever thy power." As long as you do retain
> the hair, the Spirit remains powerless over that per-
> son.

I remembered the night I had seen Miss Barton leaving my bedroom, and I thought of the lock of hair I had
just seen in her locket. I closed the ledger and went to her
room. I opened the door without knocking. Miss Barton
was lying on her bed, and she sat up quickly as I entered the
room. I went quickly to her dresser, opened the drawer,
and took out the locket.

She made no attempt to stop me. "You don't need that,"
she said. "Your life will be better without it."

"A life like yours?"

"Any kind of life you want, Elizabeth."

"And what if I should want to have an extraordinary
life?"

"There are many ways of doing that. I'll help you."

"It isn't your help I want. Frances will help me. She has
never told me what to do or believe. She is not concerned
with right and wrong, as you are, but just with what I am.
You should understand how important that is. Haven't we
allowed you to be what you are here?"

Miss Barton sat on the edge of the bed. She was silent.

As I watched her I saw a vague movement out of the
corner of my eye. I turned to face the mirror. Frances was
smiling at me.

As I left the room Miss Barton said, "Don't forget your grandmother, Elizabeth."

I went to the attic, where I could be alone with Frances. She had never looked happier.

"Have you missed me, my cony?" she said.

"Yes. Oh yes."

"I warned you there was danger in that woman."

"I didn't think she could have control over you."

"Ours is not the only power, Elizabeth. You must always beware the others."

"Do you know what has become of my grandmother?"

"I know of nothing in this house since I was banished."

"Grandmother has disappeared. I thought it was our doing."

"No. I was watching Martha from the glass in her chamber, waiting for you to perform the ritual, when I was taken from you."

"Can you help me find out what happened to her?"

"No. That is for the cunning folk to tell you."

I told her about my visit to John Dickson's. "He said you were responsible, but he showed me Uncle James's face. Do you have any connection with him?"

Frances laughed. "No. I do not visit men."

"Maybe I should forget the matter. We should be thinking about the future."

"No. Do not forget what has happened. I told you to beware the others. You should know your enemies and rivals. You have the strength to protect yourself now. Proceed."

James joined us in the attic later. He was delighted to find me in such good spirits. The three of us were delighted. Before he left, James told me he had arranged for the two of us to go to Lake George. We would leave in the morning.

When I returned to my room I found Keith asleep on my bed. Next to him was one of his snakes, the scarlet king he called Martha.

The bathroom door was closed, and from behind it I heard a sound that resembled the crying of a child. I went to the door and opened it. Mr. Scratch was backed against the tiled wall, his eyes vividly reflecting the light from the bedroom. He arched his back and spit at me. I turned the bathroom light on and closed the door.

I went to the bed and shook Keith. He opened his eyes and looked at me confusedly. "Keith," I said. "You must get that snake out of here. It's terrifying the cat."

"It won't hurt the cat," he said.

"What are you doing here, anyway?"

"Mother says I can't go to the lake with you. Can you get her to change her mind?"

"You have to go to school."

"I can take a couple of days off. I want to look for snakes."

"You stay here with your mother. I'll find a snake for you."

"You don't know where to look."

"Mr. Hurlbut will help me. We'll find something uncommon. Believe me."

Keith looked even younger than usual. His lower lip curled downward in a childish, unattractive pout. He displeased me, but I took him in my arms. "Go to bed now," I said. The cat was still yowling in the bathroom. It needed my comfort more than Keith did.

I put my hand on the snake, and it reluctantly began to move. Its distended body showed that it had been fed very recently. I draped its cold, luridly colored body around Keith's neck, took the boy's hand, and led him to the door.

"We'll talk in the morning," I said.

When he was gone I opened the bathroom door and

picked up Mr. Scratch. "Come," I said. "See Frances." I took him to the mirror, and he quickly calmed down.

Frances was watching us carefully. "Do you like him?" I asked her.

"Yes, my dear. He's a sensitive creature, an ally."

I put the cat on the bed. Avoiding the spot where the snake had been, he moved to the pillow next to mine and stretched out to watch me as I took my clothes off. Frances said goodnight to me, and her image faded from the mirror.

I was unable to sleep that night. The doubts and confusions—the slight weakness, perhaps—that I had felt in recent days had left me. I felt confidence and strength suffusing my mind and body the way waves of giddiness arrive after one has had too much to drink. I recalled a night when I was still a child. Father and I were alone, and he had drunk so much that he forgot I was a child—his child. I asked him why he drank so much. He handed me the large glass of whiskey he was holding.

"There is only one way to explain," he said.

As I sipped the whiskey he put a record on the phonograph and began to dance. The music was Ravel's *La Valse*, I think, and I listened and watched carefully as I drank. I felt pleasure rise in me as my usual perception of the room and of my father altered. I understood, though, that there was weakness and helplessness in that pleasure. I don't think Father ever understood that simple truth, even at the times he stumbled and fell, as he did while dancing that night.

I finished the whiskey while he lay on the floor moaning and twitching occasionally. The music had ended, and the needle was thumping back and forth against the record label when Mother arrived home. Her face was pale as she looked at us. Her lips, which were parted in anger, were also pale. I remembered that she had been wearing dark-red lipstick when she went out that night.

She slapped me and poured whiskey over Father's face.

It was an instructive evening. It was the evening I came to understand my parents and to realize that consciousness was not unalterable, but could grow into many forms. Later I learned that some of those forms bestowed strength.

I could feel the strength within me now as I lay waiting for the dawn. At some point during the night I rose from the bed and went to the dresser. I picked up a lipstick and drew a carefully proportioned circle on the mirror. Inside the circle I wrote "Martha," the name of Keith's snake.

Keith didn't speak to me or to anyone else at breakfast the next morning. Martha, his scarlet king snake, had died during the night. I touched Miss Barton's locket, which lay against my chest, and tried not to smile.

There was a feeling of anticipation at the table. I knew that the next time I sat at that table I would be surrounded by happy people, but I wondered whether they would be the same people.

Miss Barton looked at me regretfully but not resentfully. She had acted out of concern for me, but not out of respect, and we both knew I would never again be able to trust her. There was no reason for her to remain with us. Her departure would hurt Katherine, who had learned more from my tutor than I had. But Katherine would be able to find new friends now that she knew where to look for them.

As James went upstairs to get our bags, I waited in the study with Miss Barton.

"How long will you be at the lake?" she asked. She spoke softly, as though she didn't want to hear the answer.

"Just a day or two," I said. "I don't suppose you'll be here when I get back."

For a moment she held her breath in surprise. "Why do you say that?"

"There are dangers in this house, aren't there?"

"Yes. But not just for me."

"Primarily for you. I wouldn't want anything to happen to you, Miss Barton."

"You once called me Anne."

"I once thought you were honest with me."

She began to weep. Her tears loosened little pieces of yellow matter that had accumulated in the inner corners of her eyes. She probably was thinking I was overlooking the love she felt for me. I wasn't overlooking it; I simply thought there was nothing admirable in it. Her love was as destructive to me as another's hate might be.

Twenty-three

James and I drove out of the city in his red sports car. Mr. Scratch was in my lap. James wanted to drive up the West Side Highway, but I made him cross over to New Jersey so that we could go through the Holland Tunnel. I liked the feeling of being beneath the gray water of the Hudson River, and I wished there had been no lights in the tunnel. When we emerged into the tangle of roadways and junk-strewn marshes on the other side of the river, I said, "I think Miss Barton will be leaving us very soon."

"Why would she do that?" James asked. He didn't seem particularly interested, but I knew he must be. The number and kind of women in the house were of great importance to him.

"I don't think she's been happy since Grandmother left us. She thinks there's been a murder. It obsesses her."

James didn't answer immediately. I wondered whether he was thinking about Grandmother. He wasn't. He said, "We'll have to find you a new tutor, then, won't we?"

"Yes," I said. "Perhaps someone a little younger."

James smiled for the first time that morning, and his foot moved down on the accelerator.

I didn't interrupt his fantasies, but closed my eyes and stroked Mr. Scratch's soft, deep fur. Soon we were into green countryside, and James reached over with his right hand and began to stroke the cat. I watched his strong hand, and I recalled why we were making the journey. The image of the descending candlestick returned to me. But it seemed unimportant. I wanted our trip to be pleasureful. There was no need to see Mr. Hurlbut or to speculate about Grandmother. I would leave the speculation to Miss Barton.

My flute case was on the narrow back seat of the car. I reached back and got it. I put the sections of the instrument together and put the cold mouthpiece to my lip. James's hand was on my thigh now, as I played Frances' melody.

We were happy. And as we reentered New York State and began to pass through hilly, forested areas, I thought of the animals that lurked there, waiting for other creatures to become careless. I was eager to walk through the woods along the lakeshore. Mr. Scratch stirred on my lap, and I knew he, too, was aware of the change in our surroundings. It might have been that he was also aware, as I was not, of more important changes that lay ahead.

We were near Albany when James pulled the car into a service station to buy some gasoline. While the tank was being filled, James went to the restroom. He knew I would stay in the car, for I had told him once that I enjoyed the feeling of mild anxiety that a full bladder produces. The thought of that amused him, he said, and I think it also excited him. Before he got out of the car he pressed his hand hard against my abdomen and smiled.

He left his wallet with me and asked me to pay for the gasoline with his credit card. I took out the card and began to read it as I waited for the attendant. When the attendant arrived he found me staring dumbly at the card. I don't know how long he had been standing at the window before I noticed him. I could think only of the card. It bore the name: James Francis Cuttner.

I was thinking of John Dickson's words: "It was the hand of Frances." What he had actually said was "the hand of *Francis.*" And when he showed me James's image he had correctly identified him as Francis. James had killed Grandmother. He had done it for the same reason I had gone to Castle Clinton that night: he hadn't wanted his mother to send me away to school. He wanted to preserve his pleasure. Or, as he thought of it, he did it because he loved me.

"Is anything the matter?"

James was beside me again in the car.

"I didn't know your middle name was Francis."

"I'm not especially proud of it. Mother used to call me that when I was a child. It's not a man's name."

We were back on the highway again, and I was recalling that Grandmother had said, "Frances is guilty." She, too, meant "Francis." What had she thought he was guilty of?

During the rest of the trip I wondered what, if anything, I was going to do with my new knowledge, for it was knowledge now, and not suspicion. By the time we reached the cabin I had decided I would let James determine my actions.

The cabin was damp and cold. The thickly foliaged evergreens that surrounded it let through almost no sunlight except on the rare days when there was a dry, warm breeze, and the cabin felt as if it were made of marble rather than wood. Often when staying there I had awakened in the middle of the night feeling that I was sleeping beneath the ground.

I had not visited the lake since the death of my parents, and I found myself thinking of them. There was surprisingly little to remember about them. It was like being reminded of a person one had sat next to in school but had never been particularly friendly with. You could remember such things as unwashed feet in worn sandals, a high-pitched nasal voice, or small, pointy teeth. But no feeling of relationship could be reconstructed. I wondered whether many people thought of their parents as more than chance guardians; how many would have chosen their parents as people they wanted to spend their early years with. Was there anyone who felt about his or her parents the way I felt about Frances? I had come to think of her as my parent. We had chosen each other, and we shared a heritage. If some day I were to have a daughter, Frances, rather than I, would be her parent.

I think James was also remembering the day my mother and father died.

"Let's go swimming," he said.

"You know I can't swim."

"I'll teach you."

He was taking his clothes off and glancing at his body in the mirror. It was the mirror in which I had first seen Frances. She was there now, smiling, and looking at me rather than at James. I pulled my sweater off and stepped out of my skirt. James helped me take off my underclothes.

"I dote on you," he said.

I wondered what he meant when he said that sort of thing. Probably just that I excited him.

"What would you do for me?" I asked.

"Anything."

"Would you hurt someone for me?"

"Anyone."

"Would you hurt yourself for me?"

James had not been taking me seriously, but now that I had challenged his courage, I knew he would. He suddenly looked self-conscious. I suppose it is difficult to feel courageous without one's clothes. He looked around the room and then went to the dresser, opened a drawer, and took out a candle. It was a tall red taper, and I had never seen one like it at the cabin before. It was the type of candle that was used in the silver holders at our house in the city.

James lit the candle and held it in his left hand. He held his right hand about a foot above the flame and gradually brought the hand closer to the candle. He was smiling and looking into my eyes.

"Tell me when you're satisfied," he said. His voice was steady.

As his hand got closer to the flame he continued to smile, but he squinted and his eyes began to water. I had no intention of asking him to stop. When the hand was two or three inches from the flame it hesitated and began to tremble. He had been sexually aroused when he began his ridiculous demonstration, but the pleasure he had found in his discomfort was leaving him now.

"Satisfied?" he asked.

I smiled and shook my head. His eyes closed and the muscles in his jaws tightened.

He threw the candle on the floor and said, "Bitch."

"I thought you loved me."

"I do, you bitch. Haven't I just proved it?"

He held the palm of his hand out to me. It was already beginning to blister. I was not sure what he had proved, but I doubted whether it was love. We went into the bathroom, and I sprayed his hand with an aerosol anesthetic. The muscles in his jaw were still tight, and I supposed the pain extended well below the surface of his hand.

"Where did the candle come from?" I asked.

I couldn't tell whether his eyes showed pain or alarm.

"You're supposed to be thinking about me, not about the damn candle."

He took my right hand in his left and led me out of the

cabin toward the dock and the small beach. "We're going swimming," he said.

I wondered whether Mr. Hurlbut would be watching us from among the trees and what our bodies would mean to him.

High black clouds had formed while we were in the cabin, and lightning flashed occasionally, too far away for us to hear any thunder. There was no wind, the lake was smooth, and the only sound was the squeaking chirp of a pair of swallows that swooped erratically over the lake.

James ran out into the water and began to swim strongly away from shore. I waded out until the cold water reached my thighs and then lowered myself slowly, hardly able to feel the sand and smooth stones against my numb body. I lay back on my elbows, keeping my head above the water. The lightning flashes became more frequent, and now the stillness was broken by occasional faint thumpings of distant thunder. I thought again of my parents, and I wondered how they had felt when the lake had closed over them. I lowered my head beneath the water and held it there as long as I could.

I was surprised to find that after the first few moments I was not aware of the water but only of my body. The only sound was the rapidly increasing pulsation of my heart, as deep and percussive as the thunder I had heard above the water. My lungs began to feel as though they were filled with ice, and I became so fully aware of them that I could see them as two intensely white shapes hovering before me. My arms and legs felt metallic: cold and heavy.

When I could bear it no longer, I raised my head and breathed deeply. The silence and the darkening sky contrasted dramatically with what I had seen and heard beneath the water. James was swimming back toward me. The world I was seeing seemed strangely placid, and I found myself attracted to the intensity of the world I had just left. I lowered my head again. Drowning was a very private way of dying, I thought: a turning in upon oneself; destruction by one's own functions.

I had breathed deeply before submerging the second time, and I stayed under much longer than I had the first time. As I was about to raise my head, I felt a pressure against my throat. It was a hand, and although it was not tight around my neck, it was strong enough to keep me from raising my head. Before I had time to panic, the pressure was released and the hand moved to my shoulder, lifting me above the water. It was James, of course. He had been holding me down with his burned hand.

"Are you satisfied?" he asked me.

Lightning struck, and almost simultaneously we heard the crash of thunder. We ran for the cabin as the sound echoed through the hills across the lake.

James lit the gas heater in the cabin. The heater's chimney pipe was wrapped with a grayish insulating material where it passed through the wall of the cabin. A small animal of some kind had chewed through the insulation. I wondered whether the animal was in the cabin with us.

Rain began to fall, hissing through the needles of the pine trees. We wrapped ourselves in towels, and I bandaged James's hand. We got into bed and lay without touching, listening to the rain. James was breathing deeply and evenly, almost asleep.

I tried to recall how he had looked after he had held my head under the water. Had he been practicing his melodramatic playfulness? Or had he been trying to demonstrate something about the nature and limits of his love? I thought death, not love, was the power James understood best. When I felt his hand on my throat I realized he possessed a strength that was more than physical. He dealt not in means, as I did, but in ends—in the ultimate end. I had been helpless against him in that moment. It was not a feeling I enjoyed.

And yet now he lay innocently at my side. I knew that I had only to get up and walk to the mirror to bring him under my control.

"James," I said.

"Hmm?"

"You told me earlier you would hurt anyone for me. Do you enjoy hurting people?"

"I haven't hurt many."

"Did you enjoy hurting Grandmother?"

He didn't move, and his breathing remained calm. I thought maybe he hadn't heard me. "You killed Grandmother, didn't you?" I asked.

"I don't mind if you want to believe that," he said. His voice was unconcerned.

"Do you think you might kill me?" I asked.

"Why would I do that?"

"I know your secret."

"I know your secret, too, Elizabeth."

"What secret?"

"I know about this." He put his hand on my thigh where my mark was. "I know you wanted to be rid of your grandmother and that you feel guilty now that she's gone. But don't feel guilty. Believe whatever extraordinary things you want to believe. I wouldn't love you if you were ordinary."

James began to kiss me. It was probably the first time his kisses had not pleased me, but I did not resist him. I let him play his games while I listened to the rain in the trees and tried to understand what he had just said to me. Did he think I was responsible for Grandmother's disappearance, or did he just want me to take the blame for what he had done? Frances and Miss Barton had said I was not responsible, but maybe they were wrong, for I felt responsible, although I did not feel guilty, as James thought I did.

I began to feel a sort of irritation that I thought might be regret. I wasn't sure what it was I regretted, though. I only knew that I was the kind of person who required a large measure of certainty in her life, and I seemed to be surrounded by people who wanted to create uncertainty in me. I wanted James to go to sleep so that I could talk to Frances. I turned my attention to James, and very soon he was in pain and making grunting sounds of appreciation.

When he fell asleep I got quietly out of bed and put my clothes on. The storm had passed and the thunder was once more in the distance. I went to the other bedroom, where my parents had spent their last night together. I stood before the mirror and watched as the image of Frances appeared. She looked haggard but intense. I had never felt her power more strongly.

"What shall I do?" I asked her.

"You have the strength, my pet. It is time to use it."

"Is it necessary?"

"Yes. You have been accused. You must respond."

Mr. Scratch jumped onto the dresser. He was holding a small gray-furred animal in his mouth—some sort of mouse, I thought. The mouse was struggling feebly. The cat shook it violently and then dropped it. The mouse lay still, breathing rapidly. It watched the cat for a moment and then began to move erratically across the dresser. Mr. Scratch stopped it with one paw, and as the mouse squeaked faintly, took its head in his mouth and closed his jaws on it. He dropped the dead body in front of me and looked into my eyes. I put my hand on his head and felt the vibrations of his heavy purring.

I looked into the mirror and saw Frances' smiling face fading in the dim light.

Twenty-four

I felt much calmer than I had, and I was very hungry. We had brought some food with us in a picnic basket, but it was still in the car. I carried the basket in and ate a piece of French bread with one of the strong cheeses James liked. The only thing we had brought to drink was wine, and I drank more of it than I was used to. The cabin seemed unusually silent to me, but as I listened I gradually became aware of small sounds in the background. James was breathing noisily in the bedroom—not quite snoring, but gulping air like a wounded animal. The wind moved the wet branches of the trees, and on the wind I heard a distant tapping sound. I went to the porch and listened more carefully. The tapping was coming from near the lake, on the adjoining property, where Mr. Hurlbut had his house. I walked toward the sound, being splashed occasionally by falling drops of cold rainwater that had accumulated in the trees. When I reached the lake I saw Mr. Hurlbut a few yards down the beach. He was swinging a large two-bladed ax, cutting the branches from a fallen tree. He was facing in my direction, and when he saw me he put the ax down.

As I approached him I wondered why Grandmother had taken him as her lover. I supposed it was for his body, which even now in his old age was impressive. It was a body that had been neglected not through disuse, as most people's are, but through reckless use. I could understand how his scars and odors might attract a woman who was accustomed to clean, smooth-skinned men.

Mr. Hurlbut stood calmly as I approached him, but his eyes were not calm. I didn't speak to him until I was standing close enough to see the white stubble on his face and throat.

"Hello, Mr. Hurlbut."

"Hello, Elizabeth." He didn't call me "miss" as he usually did. "You just get here, did you?"

"Yes. Uncle James and I drove up."

"Uh-huh." Speech was not easy for him. The sounds he made seemed to surprise him, the product of an unfamiliar act. But he didn't seem unwilling to talk. He had something to say. I sat down on the trunk of the fallen tree and waited while he decided how to say it. When he was still silent after a minute or two, I said, "I was surprised when you came to visit Grandmother."

He frowned and cleared his throat. "Did she tell you I visited?"

"No. I saw you."

"Did she have a talk with you?"

"No."

His frown deepened.

"Grandmother has vanished," I said.

His eyes widened, and he looked around as though he wasn't sure who had spoken. He looked at me again and said, "How do you mean, vanished?"

"You didn't know?"

"How would I know?"

"James was up here to look for her. I thought he would have talked to you about it."

Mr. Hurlbut sat down next to me. "How do you mean, vanished?" he repeated.

"There's nothing much to tell. She just disappeared the night after your visit. We don't know how."

Mr. Hurlbut got up suddenly and reached for the ax. He raised it and brought it down viciously against the tree trunk. It was the kind of angry gesture James might have made, and it convinced me more than any words might have that Mr. Hurlbut had not known about the disappearance.

"What did you say to Grandmother?" I asked.

"It's that boy," he said.

"What boy?"

The old man sat down next to me again and stared at the ground. Five minutes must have passed. There was a large black ant on my leg, moving frantically and stopping occasionally as if in confusion. A thrush sang in the depths of the woods. Finally Mr. Hurlbut said, "You're not a child any more, are you?"

"Of course not."

"That means I oughtn't to trust you. But there's no one else."

I put my hand on his, which he clenched and moved away.

"What do you think of your Uncle James?"

"He's very good to me."

"He's not good *for* you, though. You ought to get away from him."

"Is that what you told Grandmother?"

He nodded, still staring at the ground.

"How can you know whether James is good or bad? You've hardly ever seen him."

"I've seen him when he didn't know it. I saw him out on the lake with your parents when they died. They'd still be alive if he hadn't been with them."

"You think James killed my parents?"

"He let them die. He helped them die."

"Why didn't you say so at the time?"

"A man doesn't speak easily against his son."

"James is your son?"

"So I'm told. I have no reason to doubt it."

I had no reason to doubt it, either. The physical resemblance between the two was obvious once it was pointed out. But Mr. Hurlbut was wrong about James and my parents.

"Why would James want to kill my parents?" I asked.

"You should know that better than anyone. He wanted you."

"James didn't kill my parents. I'm sure of that."

"You're wrong, Elizabeth. James is not a good man."

"It's you who are wrong," I said.

It was not difficult to imagine how he had come to feel a resentment against his son. James had lived in another world—had shared that world with the woman Mr. Hurlbut presumably loved. I turned my head to look at him—a man who had grown old in a world of natural violence. He had seen trees split by lightning. He had heard animals squeal in the night, had found their bloodied bodies among the trees at dawn. He had told his wife of what he had seen and had smiled as she silently turned away, biting her gray lips.

"Why are you telling me this?" I asked.

"There's no one else to tell. I can't let him do more harm. Before now, I didn't think he'd injure you. I just thought you'd be better off away from him. I didn't want him punished. I just asked his mother to send you off to school. But if he hurt his mother, there's nothing he wouldn't do."

I remembered James holding my head under the water. "And what do you want me to do?"

"Stay with me," he said. His face was distorted in the light of the sunset. Most of the clouds had cleared and the sky was a brilliant pink that reflected in the rippling water like the pulsing light from a defective neon sign. "Stay at my place, at least for now, while I go and see James."

"What will you do to him?"

"I'll find out what became of his mother."

"Let me talk to him first," I said. "He'll tell me things he wouldn't tell you. I'll come and see you tomorrow and let you know what I've learned. We can decide then what we should do."

Mr. Hurlbut was trembling. I put my arm across his shoulder and kissed his cheek. I was sure it had been many years since he had been so close to a young woman.

"Martha," he whispered.

He was thinking of Grandmother. I wondered whether he was thinking of her as she was when he last saw her or as she was before James was born. I put both my arms around him and lowered his head against my chest. He leaned against me awkwardly but gratefully, as an injured child might, conscious primarily of his pain but pleased that someone else was aware of it. He was too weak to deal with James.

The sun had moved below the crest of the mountain as we sat in our uneasy embrace. As the darkness increased, Mr. Hurlbut stopped trembling. He changed his position, and it became obvious that he had stopped grieving for Martha.

"It's all right," I said. "It's all right. We're not really related."

When I returned to the cabin, James was in the kitchen. In one hand he held a glass of whiskey and in the other a half-eaten scallion. Crumbs were lodged in the hair of his bare chest.

"Where have you been?" he asked me.

"Just walking. Watching the sunset."

"I thought maybe you were performing a little moonlight ritual."

As I had expected, now that he had mentioned my "secret," he would not be able to keep quiet about it. There was no need for me to reply to him. There were more direct ways than speech to teach him the truth.

"I ran into Mr. Hurlbut," I said.

James was not interested enough to answer. He bit into the scallion. As he chewed, his eyes watered slightly.

"We had an interesting conversation."

"I didn't know he was capable of conversation—and certainly not interesting conversation. I thought he communicated by means of odors."

"You don't feel any affinity for him?"

"Only a mild repulsion. Although Mother was always interested in him, I think."

"He hadn't known about her disappearance. He was upset when I mentioned it."

"I suppose you told him I was responsible."

"I didn't have to. He's a perceptive man."

"Not about people, he isn't—only about storms and snakes."

James finished his drink and refilled the glass.

"Keith wants us to bring him back a snake," I said. "Maybe Mr. Hurlbut can find one for us."

"I'll find one."

"He wants a kind he doesn't have."

"Does he have a rattler?"

"No. Should he have?"

"He's careful. And they're all over the mountain. We'll get one in the morning."

"*You'll* get one."

James smiled. His smile had been created by a ridiculously expensive dentist whose office he visited often. He explained to me once that he didn't particularly care about his teeth but it pleased him to have an attractive young woman put her fingers in his mouth. James's motives were seldom what they seemed to be. His true motives were as unattractive as the little stumps that lay beneath his porcelain caps.

Twenty-five

I found James on the porch the next morning, stripping bark from a long forked stick. "I'm ready for the vipers," he said. "Are you coming along?"

"No, thanks."

My refusal pleased him and added to his obvious excitement. I seldom showed fear or distaste over anything he suggested, and he was taking advantage of this opportunity to feel superior and to demonstrate his courage. He put some chocolate in his pocket and took a pillowcase to carry his trophy in. When he was ready to leave, he came to me and put his hands on my shoulders. He had wanted to kiss me, but as he looked into my eyes, he hesitated. He started to speak.

"Well . . ."

But he said no more. He picked up his stick and walked toward the mountain. Mr. Scratch followed him, moving stealthily along the edge of the path. I went to the bedroom, where Frances awaited me. I stood for a few minutes, staring at her and feeling a strength rise within me. She had a reality for me that I could find nowhere else, and I regretted I could not be with her constantly. Soon we would be closer. Soon I would be the only person of significance in the building on Coenties Slip, and I could devote all of my time to Frances. Perhaps I would learn to touch her. Perhaps I would be able to awaken in the middle of the night and feel her body against mine. Her skin would be cool and dry.

"It is time to draw the circle," Frances said.

I reached out toward the mirror and put my hand against its surface. The glass was not flat, but was indented slightly over her reflection like a very shallow relief carving. I pressed the surface and felt it give way slightly under my fingers.

"The circle, my sweet," she said. "There will be time for touching."

Her image was slightly blurred. There were tears in my eyes.

I walked along the water's edge toward a small circular gazebo that stood on a rocky point. The structure had been neglected for years. Its shingled roof had collapsed in places and its unpainted wood had weathered and decayed. It could have been the skeleton of some improbable creature that had crawled out of the lake to die. I stepped carefully onto the rotted floor, which was about six feet in diameter. I could make out a few initials that had been carved into the gray posts and railings. I thought of lovers who had stood, or perhaps lain, here years ago. It was possible that Grandmother and Mr. Hurlbut were among them.

I had brought along a plastic pail, which I had filled with sand from our beach. I stood in the center of the floor and took a handful of the sand, holding out my arm and letting the sand spill slowly through my fingers. I repeated the motion, turning slowly around until a circle of sand surrounded me. Then, within the circle, I shaped more sand into the name "James Francis Cuttner." When I had finished, I stood for a moment, thinking of James. I imagined him walking through the woods, looking under rock ledges and probing into sheltered pits. I began to shiver violently and found myself saying words that I didn't recognize. As my voice became uncontrollably louder, I began to perspire. My skin prickled and the sky seemed suddenly dark. The last thing I remembered before losing consciousness was a hollow, yowling sound that might have been made by a sexually aroused cat.

I opened my eyes briefly and then closed them once more against the strong light. I could smell rotting wood and there was sand in my mouth. When I could keep my eyes open, I raised myself slowly from the floor of the gazebo and stood for a moment, clinging to one of its posts. The sun was low above the mountains to the west. I moved carefully out of the gazebo and started back to the cabin.

Mr. Hurlbut was sitting on the porch. He didn't get up as I approached him, but he was obviously relieved to see me. He had shaved, and although he wore the same dirt-stiffened clothes he had worn yesterday, he seemed cleaner. I supposed he had bathed last night, sitting in the black-ringed tub while his wife waited in the next room, listening to the splashing water, wondering what regrettable thing had happened or was about to happen.

"I fell asleep," I said.

"Where is he?"

"James? Isn't he back yet? He went to Tongue Mountain to hunt for a snake for Keith."

"When did he go?"

"This morning. Early."

Mr. Hurlbut got up and said, "I'd better go after him."

"But it will be dark soon."

"I'll get a light. We can't leave him out there all night."

"How will we know where to look?"

"You'll stay here. I'll try the main trail tonight. It's blazed. If I don't have any luck, I'll get some help in the morning."

"Do you think he's lost?"

"If he's lucky, he's lost. He could be snakebit."

"How serious would that be?"

"Not bad if he got treatment right away. Bites seldom kill, and there's a few snakebite kits mounted on trees along the trail. Kids take the stuff from them, though." He looked at me blankly. "It's too bad you fell asleep," he said.

When I didn't answer him, he continued: "Do you want to stay here or at my place?"

"I want to come with you."

Surprisingly, he didn't argue with me.

"It won't be comfortable," he said. "And you'll need some high boots."

"I think there are some in the cabin that fit me. Heavy rubber."

He started toward his cabin. "I'll be back soon," he said.

Frances was pleased. "You did well, my sweeting," she said as she watched me change my clothes. I wanted to press my body against the mirror.

Mr. Hurlbut was wearing high leather boots. He carried a large battery-powered lantern, a red-and-white box, and the same kind of forked stick that James had taken with him. He handed me the box. "It's a first-aid kit," he said. "Stay about a yard behind me."

We walked quickly into the dark woods, following the brilliant bluish light of the lantern. The trail was wide and familiar to me at first, but it gradually became steep and barely perceptible. Finally I could see no sign that anyone had walked there before. Mr. Hurlbut began tilting the lantern upward, picking out metal blazing tags that had been attached to trees. I stumbled occasionally in my clumsy boots, and branches of bushes and trees scratched my face. I held my forearm in front of my head to protect my eyes. Insects whined about me, and I slapped my neck, bringing my hand away marked with my bright blood and the crushed body of a mosquito.

We suddenly reached a clearing at the edge of a cliff. Full darkness had fallen, and I could hear the lake sloshing against rocks far below us. Mr. Hurlbut sat down and turned off the lantern.

"Did he come this way?" I asked.

"Someone did. I think he kept moving off the trail, though. We could have passed him already."

We sat in silence for a few minutes. I wondered what Mr. Hurlbut was hoping to find—whether his desire to avenge Martha's death was stronger than whatever feeling he might have for his son. He needn't have made the search in the darkness. Did he want to help James, or was he only hoping to see him in distress?

Mr. Hurlbut switched the lantern back on. "Do you hear anything unusual?" he asked.

I listened carefully, but I heard only the sound of the water, the wind in the trees, and the faint whine of an outboard motor from across the lake. Then I heard another, fainter sound.

"Yes," I said. "What is it?"

"It's a cat. A house cat, I think."

He stood up and started off in the direction of the sound. I followed, but more hesitantly than before. As the sound grew louder, I recognized it as the same yowling I had heard earlier at the gazebo. It was Mr. Scratch, I was certain.

We were still following the trail, and I thought we must have been near the top of the mountain. Even though the mountain was not much more than a big hill, and despite its gradual incline, I was beginning to feel tired. My clothes were wet with perspiration.

Mr. Hurlbut stopped and held the light steadily on a spot ahead of him. A pair of luminous green-yellow eyes reflected back at us for a moment and then vanished quickly. I saw a flash of reddish fur move out of the circle of light. And then I noticed something else. Emerging from a rocky depression ahead of us was a hand. We moved slowly forward, and as we reached higher ground we saw a swollen, grimacing face next to the hand. It was a lifeless face. It was James's face.

His eyes were open and his mouth was twisted as though he were crying out. He looked like a drowning man struggling to keep his face above the water and reaching out to touch the air for the last time. I remembered the opera we had seen together. In the circle of light from the lantern, James looked like the spotlighted Don Giovanni being dragged down into the underworld to his death.

Mr. Hurlbut went forward, but I turned away and waited for him to return. I was still carrying the first-aid kit, but I knew it would not be needed. I heard Mr. Hurlbut struggling to move the body, and it was ten minutes before he returned and stood behind me.

"We might as well go back. I'll get someone to help bring him down in the morning."

We moved awkwardly down the mountain, unspeaking, while above us curious night creatures must have sniffed and nudged James's cold, bloated flesh.

I stayed in Mr. Hurlbut's cabin that night. We consoled each other as incomprehensible speech came from behind the door of his wife's bedroom.

Twenty-six

Katherine didn't weep on the afternoon of her husband's funeral, but that evening, when she, Keith, and I sat in the dining room at Coenties Slip, she stared at Miss Barton's empty chair, tears falling onto her uneaten food.

Miss Barton had packed her shabby suitcase when James and I left for the lake and had returned to the place she had come from. The note she left on Katherine's bed didn't say where that place was. We were free of her meddling, and although Katherine was disturbed, she would discover that I had qualities that would more than replace those she had found so fascinating in Miss Barton. I would let her make the discovery herself, though, and I made no attempt to interfere with her dull distraction. The days were placid.

The nights, however, were exciting. I spent them with Frances. We did not speak of my life, but of hers and of the lives of others who had followed her. Each night she became more palpable to me. As she spoke I would run my fingertips over the mirror, which had become something warm and pliant.

Mr. Cuttner often had dinner with us. He was generous and attentive, but not offensively so. I began to realize that he was interested in us but did not love us. I doubted that he had ever loved anyone, and I admired him for that. He had perhaps come closer to loving objects than he had to loving people. That seemed a harmless enough attitude, since things are not corrupted by the emotions of those who own or use them.

Keith had sold his snakes, perhaps because of what had happened to his father, but more likely because his needs were becoming more complex. He asked me if I would leave my bathroom door ajar when I bathed, and he had begun to hum tunes from *Don Giovanni,* his thin, cracking voice becoming firmer each week.

I thought often of John Dickson and of his stark apartment. I wondered whether he would like to live amid the elaborate furnishings of the house on Coenties Slip.

I seldom thought of James.

I don't know exactly when I began to have the dream. It didn't disturb me especially, because I have always had elaborate dreams. From the time I was a child one of my great pleasures was to lie in bed after awakening and recall the images that had been given me as I slept. I thought of them as gifts, but I never tried to imagine who the giver might be.

The new dream was always basically the same. I was an infant: tiny, naked, sexless, and rigid, like an old-fashioned doll. I was lying in an expanse of deep black weeds. My eyes and head were immobile, and I stared fixedly into the space above me, which was transparent, but heavy and distorting, like a block of imperfect glass. I would hear a harsh, animallike breathing and a rustling in the weeds at my side. Gradually, two heads moved into my line of vision. The heads, which grew out of a reptilian body, were those of Frances and Miss Barton. The creature straddled me, and the heads descended, with dry, pale tongues protruding. The tongues began to lick my body, scraping against me with a rasping sound. Under the abrasive, rhythmic, ceaseless caress of the tongues, my body began to diminish, as though it were a block of hard cheese being finely torn by the teeth of a steel grater. Gradually my features were leveled, my arms and legs became stubs, and my torso was reduced to a constantly shrinking, less definite shape. Finally I was reduced to nothingness, and a darkness descended, engulfing the four glowing eyes of the creature.

I told no one, not even Frances, of the dream. One of the nice things about dreams is that no one else knows you have them. I didn't think of what the dream might mean. It would have been pointless, for dreams have no meaning for the dreamer. It is always others who "interpret" and find meaning in them.

But the images disturbed me. They recurred each night, and if I sat quietly in the daytime, I heard the panting breath and the rustling of the weeds. Although I didn't really regret Miss Barton's absence, I began to recall how useful she had been in helping to pass the hours of the mornings and afternoons. I reminded myself, however, that she had once deprived me of my special qualities; that although she had been occasionally diverting, she had been a constant danger.

The evenings became the best time of day for me, and

after dinner I went immediately to my room, where I could speak to Frances. I gave less and less of my time to sleep, sitting before the mirror and Frances until consciousness left me and was replaced by the dream. After the dream I would force my eyes to open for a few minutes before the dream began again.

It was a night after I had awakened from the dream that my life was changed.

My eyes had opened quickly, and in the dim light of the room I saw a figure standing at the dresser. It seemed at first to be Frances, and a pleasant excitement swept over me. Had she finally freed herself from the mirror? Nothing could have pleased me more. As I was about to stand up and go to her, I realized it was not Frances. It was Miss Barton, and she was holding her locket—the locket that she had used to deprive me of my power. It still contained the cuttings of my hair. I knew I must not let her leave the room, but I felt immobilized. She looked at me briefly, with an expression that combined sympathy and distaste, and then she turned and hurried from the room.

A few moments passed before I could force myself to my feet. I knew that unless I regained the locket, I might be deprived of my heritage forever. And I might never see Frances again. I went to the mirror. Frances was not there.

I ran to the hallway.

"Miss Barton? Anne? Come back . . . please come back." I was shouting uncontrollably.

I went into her old room and turned on the lights. The room was empty and cold. I looked into her mirror and saw only my own tear-dampened face.

"Frances? Don't leave me."

I ran up the stairs to the attic, calling for Miss Barton. I climbed over the old, heavy furniture that was stored there, pulling off dust covers and looking into any space in which Miss Barton might have been concealed. Dust rose about me, swirling in the dim light, choking and blinding me. I groped my way to the unrolled rug on which James and I had spent so many hours. The old mirror glinted before me, and as I stared into it I heard a terrifying scream. In an instant the glass collapsed into slivers and jagged fragments.

I stood quietly as the dust settled about me, and I stared at the pieces of slivered glass that reflected random areas of the attic and its contents: uncovered ceiling beams; the faded tapestry covering of a chair; the folds of my nightgown.

Then I saw a flash of motion in one large piece of the mirror, and when the movement stopped I saw a face. It was Katherine.

"Elizabeth," she said. "What's happened?"

I turned toward the door, where Katherine stood. She looked as if she was ready to run from me at any moment.

"Have you seen Miss Barton?" I asked.

"No. Has she been here?"

Katherine backed away from the doorway slightly. Her thick shoulders were mottled under the twisted straps of her nightgown. She looked as gross and ineffectual as ever, but there was a trace of life in her eyes that I had not seen since Miss Barton had left us.

As I moved toward the door, Katherine stepped back again. "I'll search the house," she said.

I knew she would find nothing. I ignored her and went to my room. I locked the door behind me and stood before the mirror. I pulled off my gown and let it fall to the floor. I leaned over the dresser and lifted the heavy mirror from its hook on the wall, carrying it carefully to my bed. I lay down beside it, smearing the glass with tears from my wet cheeks, feeling its coldness against my body.

"Frances," I whispered.

Some time later Katherine knocked on the door and called to me. I didn't answer her that night or the following day. Eventually I heard her say, "Elizabeth, a doctor is here to see you."

I heard metal being scraped against the lock of the bedroom door. I held the mirror closer to my body.

Twenty-seven

The doctor came to see me almost every day. I found no reason to say anything to him. He called himself Dr. Stafford, and he smiled frequently, revealing remarkably large, unclean teeth. He had thick, hairy wrists, and he wore three rings. I think he was an unhappy man.

He met me in what he called my sitting room. I couldn't remember how I came to be in those rooms, and I despised them. I thought longingly of the polished wood and intricately patterned carpets in the house at Coenties Slip. I believe everything in my new rooms was made of plastic or metal, and nothing was decorated. Even the people who came to ask me questions or to bring me food wore plain white or pale green. I was not allowed to have a mirror.

I did speak to Dr. Stafford once. I told him the things I have told you. He listened solemnly and attentively, looking not at me but at a pad of yellow paper on which he wrote with a faintly squeaking green pen. I wasn't surprised that he didn't believe what I told him. I think he was paid to persuade people to be as ordinary as he was.

The doctor believed I was mistaken about the things that happened to me after my parents' death. When he visited me, he spoke of what he called the "truth."

Although I did not speak to Dr. Stafford, I often thought of what he said to me during his visits. He had just a few set speeches, which he delivered with pretended conviction.

His voice was quiet but tense, and as he spoke he held his old-fashioned green fountain pen, wrapping his fingers around its barrel and pressing his thumb against the end of its cap. He always concluded by assuring me that everyone in the family loved me. I was expected to believe that James committed desperate acts for me; that he murdered first my parents and then Grandmother to keep me near him. Apparently all those who are involved would rather believe in illegal but conventionally explainable acts than in something they think of as supernatural. They would rather have a murderer in the family than a witch.

Supposedly, Mr. Hurlbut claims he saw James either drown my parents or refuse to rescue them. And Mr. Cuttner now says he saw James take Grandmother's body from the house that night and put it in the trunk of his car. Both men remained silent at first because they wanted to protect the man each of them thought of as a son. It was believed that James buried Grandmother at Lake George when he drove up there the following day. Her body had not been found, but that did not alter their beliefs. I admitted they could be right about James and Grandmother, but I was not convinced.

Dr. Stafford did what was expected of him. He prepared a complex but commonplace explanation of the situation. The explanation was less interesting to me than anything else he spoke of. He seemed to be fascinated with the concept of guilt. He wanted me to believe that because I didn't love my parents I wanted to punish myself by accepting responsibility for their death, and that I imagined Frances and her power as a means of assuming the responsibility.

The doctor didn't speak of good and evil, but he might have been more convincing if he had. He expected of me exactly what ignorant men expected centuries ago: confession and recantation.

I was sure my determination would exceed his patience.

And if it did not, there was a factor he had not anticipated. I was going to have a child.

I'm not sure what I thought about becoming a mother. At first I took some consolation in the thought that the powers taken from me would not be lost, but would live on in my child. But that thought did not comfort me very long. I suppose most parents think of their children as an offering that will somehow absolve them of responsibility for their own failings. That was not enough for me. I soon realized that it would be intolerable to watch my child assume a power I no longer possessed.

I had to regain that power.

Twenty-eight

The doctor soon discovered that I was pregnant. He smiled at me continually after that, but I still did not speak to him.

He immediately brought Katherine to see me. She had visited me a few times after I left the house on Coenties Slip, but I found her company depressing. She would sit staring vapidly at the plastic floor, breaking our silence only to speak of Miss Barton, who apparently telephoned occasionally, without saying where she was living.

I pictured Miss Barton in a rooming house, gazing at the ceiling, lying alone on a stained mattress, the locket resting between her slack breasts. She probably wondered why her betrayal of me brought her so little satisfaction. I wondered whether she regretted what she did to me. Someday she would feel regret, I was sure. She would feel it intensely.

There was a change in Katherine's manner in that visit. At first I was aware only that she was talking more than usual. Then I noticed that she was smiling in the same way the doctor had been smiling. I began to realize the value my pregnancy might have. The doctor and Katherine had begun to think of me in more ordinary terms now that I was in a condition that the most ordinary of women eventually find themselves in. It was then I knew that my salvation lay in the appearance of normality.

Katherine and I were seated facing each other. I raised my head and gave her my full attention. She smiled eagerly and stupidly. I rose and walked to her chair. I took her hair in my hands and held her head against my belly.

"Do you hear my daughter's heart beating?" I asked.

Katherine's head trembled against my body. She raised her arms, and I felt her uneven fingernails pressing into my buttocks through the thin material of my robe and gown.

"Oh, my darling," she said. "You're back with us."

"Yes," I said.

The front of my robe was stained with Katherine's tears.

Katherine began to visit me twice a day, probably in the hope of once again feeling my belly against her cheek. I gave her only my words.

I began to talk to the doctor. He was a most ordinary man, with ordinary beliefs. He was extraordinarily insecure, however, and he thought of people who did not share his simple beliefs as "patients" whom he must "treat." A patient who agreed to accept the doctor's beliefs was pronounced "cured," as I was sure I soon would be.

"Yes, Doctor," I would say. "I can see now that I have been misguided. I must forget the past. I must learn to love."

His gratitude for my words was intense. Tears filled his eyes.

I hoped I would be allowed to go home soon. There was too much weeping where I was.

Twenty-nine

"I have a surprise for you, Elizabeth."

Katherine and I stood at the entrance to the house on Coenties Slip. A light rain was falling, softening the soot-darkened crust of a previous snowfall.

"A surprise?"

"Yes. A pleasant surprise."

The door opened. Mr. and Mrs. Taylor stood in the rich, deep shadows of the foyer. There had been no true shadows where I had been—only the slight graying of colors that passes for shadow in strong fluorescent light.

Mr. Taylor said, "Welcome home, Miss Elizabeth." He and his wife had similar expressions: a blend of curiosity and fear.

I smiled and walked past them to the full-length mirror that was mounted on the hall closet door. It was good to be home.

A voice I didn't recognize said, "Hello, Elizabeth." Over my shoulder in the mirror I saw Keith. Although his voice was deeper and firmer than it had been previously, his appearance had changed only slightly. He looked like a person who had just made some unpleasant discoveries about himself and wanted to tell someone about them.

"Hello, Keith," I said. "We must have a talk soon."

Katherine took my arm and led me away. "Your surprise is in the study," she said. "Why don't you go there alone?"

I walked to the study. The door was closed, and I hesitated a moment before opening it. I wondered whether the surprise would please me as much as it obviously pleased Katherine. I turned the handle and let the door swing open.

Miss Barton stood in the center of the room. She raised

her right arm toward me and slowly opened her hand. In it was the locket she had taken from me.

"I want to return this to you," she said.

"Why?"

"I've been unhappy."

"You were always unhappy," I said.

"Not always." She thrust the locket toward me. "Will you take it?" she asked.

"You may put it on me." I took off my coat and turned my back to her, facing the mirror in which I had so often watched Frances. Miss Barton stood behind me, unreflected in the mirror, her breath warm on my neck, her hands trembling. As she fastened the clasp, she began to sob. I ignored her sobs, for I was listening to another, fainter sound. It was a whisper:

"My cony. My sweet."

Gradually the image of Frances began to form in the mirror. She had never been so beautiful.

"Never leave me again," I said.

"No, my dear, I shan't. We are safe now."

We smiled at each other for a long time. Finally Frances said, "I shall return. You must speak with that one now." Her image faded, and I became conscious again of Miss Barton's sobs. I turned and led her to the sofa, and we sat together until she was quiet.

"And what now?" I asked her.

"May I stay with you? I could care for your child."

"There would be no point unless you approved of me. Unless you could raise the child as I want."

"You have my approval, Elizabeth. And I want yours. I want to be your sister, your helper."

"You will accept your heritage again?"

"I've done that already."

"And do you think we are evil?"

"Not necessarily. We merely have a power. Just as James

had a power. His was a natural power, and ours might be considered supernatural. But they are both human powers that can be used to achieve any human ends. We are neither more nor less evil than anyone else. We are merely human."

I pretended to be impressed by what Miss Barton had said. She could think of our powers as merely human if she chose to, but that was nonsense. However, it was not a kind of nonsense that threatened me.

While she was making her little speech I tried to decide why she had returned. Perhaps she was in love with me. Perhaps she thought my child could substitute for the one she would never have. Her reason didn't matter, however. I wanted our house to be a happy one, and she could help with that.

Thirty

And now each night I lie with my hands on my thickening body, humming the melody that Frances taught me. The activity of the house is organized around me. Or, more exactly, it is organized around the life that is developing within me.

And I am disturbed. For I think Frances is the only one who realizes that the child is only a symbol of the power that is within me. Perhaps if there were no child, their understanding of me would increase.

You understand me, don't you? I'm sure you do. That's why I have told you my story. I picture you as having hairless arms and small white teeth. Sometimes when you are alone in your car, driving along the river at dusk, you glance at the back seat, thinking you might see someone entirely different from the people you see at the office or at your dinner table.

You understand why I am rising awkwardly from my bed now and walking to the mirror and saying, "Frances. You once caused the death of a child, didn't you?"

And you understand why Frances is smiling at me.

CPSIA information can be obtained
at www.ICGtesting.com
Printed in the USA
BVHW030255140219
540188BV00003B/324/P